To Craig
with love,
xxx xxx

Changing Lives

L.J.B FRASER

Dedication

To all the women out there who are struggling with their lives. You can change it, believe in yourself. You are not alone, just ask.

There is always spring after the winter and a rainbow after the rain. It can be difficult sometimes to see the blue sky because of the dark clouds, but it's there.

Contents

Acknowledgements

There are many people who have made this book possible, too many to mention. The team at Acorn with all the support and tireless nudging to get me to each stage. I'd like to thank Leila Dewji, my wonderful editor who has encouraged me right from the start.

This has been a family affair too, so thanks to my two sons, Doug for his design input and Aly for his tireless proofreading. Doug's wife, Kirsty, and Al's partner, Jo, for allowing them to take time to help their mum. My daughter, Sarah, for being there at the end of the phone to offer encouragement and give big cuddles when my spirit was flagging. And of course my grand-daughter, Skye, for offering wisdom beyond her years to keep me going. Even though she won't be reading this book until she is a lot older. I'd like to thank my brother, John, who lives so far away, but was candid when he told me to, "Just get on with it, write the book instead of talking about it," many years ago.

My other half, Bobby, for his love and support during a very difficult time while I was juggling work, writing, moving house and just making me laugh and being there for me. And to all my friends who have believed in me, without them I wouldn't have re-built my shattered confidence and carried on.

And for all the ghosts in my past, without whom this book wouldn't have been possible.

A special thanks to Edinburgh Women's Aid and their sister services. The help I've had from them has been amazing and I'm so pleased to be giving something back to them with the sales of every book, so thank you reader, for buying this copy.

Chapter 1

THE PAST, 1989

It had been a long few weeks. The planning had all come together and a successful evening, enjoyed by all, was now at an end. She'd managed to keep the whole thing a secret from him and the look on his face as he walked into the function suite to be greeted by all their friends, proved she'd been successful. She'd got his mum and dad, brother and sister-in-law down from Aberdeen to Edinburgh to add to the surprise and had thought it would be good to meet up with them the following day for lunch. Thirtieth birthdays only come around once, and she was glad she'd been able to do something nice for her husband. The kids had enjoyed it too. Janey glowed as she remembered the look on his face when he realised what was happening. How he kissed her, laughing and dancing all evening and the beautiful words he'd said about her when the crowd had all encouraged him to say something.

Maybe this would be a turning point for them; maybe he'd realise just how much she loved him. She settled the children in bed; they were all exhausted after all the fun and a late night. She came back down the stairs and poured herself a small drink. She deserved it. She waited for him to come into the house after seeing his family off to the local bed and breakfast.

The door closed behind him and he came into the lounge and shut the door.

"Kids asleep?" he asked.

"Sound as a pound, they're exhausted." Janey turned to him, smiling and waiting for him to take her in his arms and thank her for such a wonderful evening.

His look was thunderous. "You lying bitch." He spat the words at her. "What the hell was all that about?"

Janey was shocked and felt the familiar racing of her heart and sick feeling in the pit of her stomach. "What do you mean, what have I done?"

"How did you manage to arrange all that without me knowing? You have no right to keep secrets. What else are you keeping quiet about? A lover maybe? Money squirrelled away? Planning to leave me? You will never survive without me; you need me to look after you and the kids. Never, ever do anything like that again." He grabbed her and held her close. As she felt his breath on her face and his fingers tightened around her arms, she feared the worst. He'd never forgive her for this and she'd pay the usual price. She felt herself tense. "You are mine, no one else will have you. Three kids, you're spoilt goods." He kissed her roughly. "No one else will ever love you the way I do. Bed."

Janey wriggled away from him, hot tears streaming down her cheeks. She didn't want to let him see her cry; it always made him worse. Bed it was, and another night of humiliation. Surely it shouldn't be like this. This should be a happy evening with lovemaking, not the prospect of sex with her too tense and trying not to cry as he carried on anyway. Again. She'd really done it this time. How could he be so wonderful to the outside world? Everyone thought he was the perfect husband and father, she had no one to tell, no one to turn to.

Sometimes things aren't what they seem...

Chapter 2

THE PRESENT, 2013

Losing their faithful seventeen-year-old Tibetan Spaniel on that hot sunny day, had shocked the whole family – the next few days seemed so empty without their little companion. After coming over to say goodbye to Gizmo, Janey's oldest two had departed for their own homes and the house seemed very empty as Janey adjusted to a dog-free house for the first time in twenty-seven years. She couldn't even bring herself to get rid of her faithful friend's collar, so she carried it around in her bag as some kind of good luck charm. Janey hoped her luck would change soon.

Fraser, her youngest, was at university now and although he had his own life to lead, he still lived with his Mum. Although twenty-one now, and constantly threatening to move out, Fraser was good fun and they got on well, like two unlikely housemates. He had never known a house without a four-legged pet, now it was just her and Fraser at home. The space was lovely, but sometimes too quiet. Her house had been a bit cramped as the kids got older but now that Donald, her oldest was away, living with Heather, a lovely lass, and most definitely one of the family, in the Borders and her daughter, Iona, was now living and working in Stirling. The house got busy on occasions when they were all at home, or when Fraser decided to have his guitar playing, boozy pals round, but that was fun and they all helped nowadays. Losing her dog was a huge milestone for Janey. Her parents had both died within a couple of years of each other, her mum just the previous year and she sometimes felt she was losing her grip. All this sorrow seemed overwhelming and she knew she'd have to do something.

"You'll need to get another dog, Mum." Fraser said.

His deep blue eyes brimmed with tears. He wore his blonde hair straight to his shoulders and now he shrugged it back and bent down to give Janey a hug. Janey loved her kids with a passion. Not in a smothering way, she was proud of the way her two eldest were making their way in the world and she knew she'd miss Fraser when he eventually left. It often felt strange in the house when he was away for a few days, but she'd get used to it. He still had two years of university left and he was so easy to live with. That's as long as she didn't dwell on the chaos behind his bedroom door. When she did occasionally venture in to retrieve plates, glasses, cups and cutlery she shuddered at the mess within.

The cultures Fraser could grow in an old glass of juice or forgotten cup of tea made her toes curl. Which was why it was easier to keep the door shut rather than nag. Every so often she'd hear Fraser clattering about long into the night, then the bin would magically fill and he'd even take the hoover upstairs. Janey knew that just like the others, he'd sort himself out once he had a place of his own. She supposed she'd been much the same as a teenager.

Fraser's big hug made the tears well up and she hugged him back, hard. She loved the easy way all of her children shared their emotions with her. It made the tough years of bringing them up on her own all the more worthwhile. She was still amazed at her two big sons, both tall and handsome, and her only five foot two. And her daughter, Iona, built like Janey, was in her twenties, small and petite but with long blonde hair Janey had always been so proud of. Janey's hair was dark and wavy, as her oldest, Donald's would have been, but he kept his unruly mop short.

She missed Donald, living as he did in the Borders with his partner, Heather. Donald has a good job as a creative illustrator and Heather was teaching music. They'd done what a lot of young folk did now and looked further than Edinburgh for jobs. She missed them dropping in for Sunday tea, a tradition she'd always tried to keep up as the children got older. It was a special time in the week where the family could catch up. Around the table would be whichever of her kids were staying along with whatever waifs and strays popped in. Janey's Sunday roasts were a legend amongst all their friends. They'd never be the same now without her wee dog begging for scraps and getting under everybody's feet until he got a tit bit.

"I can't get another dog just yet, Fraser, it's far too soon. And anyway, you'll not be here for much longer and dogs are quite a tie. I'd like to be able to visit your brother or sister without worrying who's looking after it." Janey pulled away from Fraser who was clearly suffering at the loss of the companion he'd had for most of his life.

"But you'll be all alone in the house," he protested, "you loved walking the dog."

"There's no law says I can't go for a walk on my own. I could join a walking group. Anyway, Katie's a great one for walking. She's always going up north bagging some Munro or other. I'm sure she thinks she'll find some handsome rich highlander one of these days."

They both smiled, Katie was Janey's friend and ever since Katie's divorce after almost twenty-five years of marriage, she was making up for lost time. All that time on the roller coaster of almost happy to miserable had made Katie determined to find her knight in shining armour. She was forever regaling stories of mad dates she'd been on. But so far, no knight.

"A walking group, mum. They're for wrinklies, and you're not really that old yet," Fraser broke into her thoughts.

"Oh, thanks very much – Katie's hardly a 'wrinkly' and she goes walking." Janey was laughing despite the threatening tears.

"But she goes with all your friends – the "Forty something Floosies.""

"So, that's what you think of us? Remember they're some of my dearest friends. And yes, we're all forty something but that doesn't mean we're all looking to jump into bed with the nearest available man."

Fraser grinned "It's about time you jumped into bed with someone mum, you'll forget how to do it soon."

Janey made a friendly swipe at him, "So cheeky for a youngest son! I don't comment on your love life."

"Speaking of which, mum, I'd better be going soon."

The twinkle in his eye made Janey think that there was more to his plans than seeing his friends gigging that evening. She was almost jealous. Not of Fraser, but of having a romantic companion. He was quite right, if she didn't do something soon, she'd heal up. She looked out of the window to the large garden beyond. "I keep thinking I'll see him bounding back from the garden at any moment. Or hear him scratching at the door to get in. I know he was old, but he was so fit, right up until the end. It seems such a shock." Fraser's eyes looked sad again.

That look made Janey's stomach clench. She knew she couldn't help him with the loss, but experience of losing other pets reminded her that things would soon feel better for him.

"He's been part of the family for seventeen years, Mum. I can't imagine the house without him. I even keep thinking I hear him rooting about in my room for scraps."

"Well don't make that an excuse for leaving the smelly plates any longer than you do now." Janey chided her son gently.

Fraser smiled, "Hint taken. But you'll miss him a lot, he's company for you when I'm not here, and besides, you'll look daft out walking on your own. You'll have no excuse to go out when I'm doing your head in."

It was Janey's turn to smile. "I'll think of some other excuse to count to ten in peace, don't you worry. Now, how about some food before I have to go out?"

"Don't worry, mum, I'll do tea. Pasta OK?"

Janey was very glad she'd encouraged all her kids to cook. There were times it came in very useful. Fraser might be a

14

midden in his bedroom, but he was very handy in the kitchen. Her mum had ruled the household when she was growing up. Her dad had been the breadwinner and the house had been her mum's domain. Even to the extent that Janey hadn't really known how to cook when she'd left home to get married. It had been a steep learning curve and she'd been determined to bring her three up to cook and iron. She had a rule in the house that everyone over the age of thirteen should do their own ironing. The ironing rule had been great; Janey didn't have too many rules, but that one had certainly saved her from the huge weekly job that so many women were a slave to. Her kids were all now experts at finding clothes that needed minimum ironing.

It was at times like this she missed her own mother. Her parents had helped her a lot with the kids when she'd finally plucked up the courage to get her abusive husband to leave. They'd been there to babysit and to help with the children after school. They were quite a close family, really. Never living on top of each other, and sorting out squabbles before they got too bad, and she even had regular contact with her brother who lived in Sydney, Australia.

Janey's mum had died a couple of years after her dad, but it was a bittersweet time for Janey. Lots of time to get to know her mum as a close friend, seeing her body get weaker, although her mind was as sharp as ever. Seeing her nearly every day. Her mum used to always tell Janey she did too much and didn't take enough time for herself. Janey remembered the huge hole her mum's death had left. Janey was glad her mum was no longer suffering but she missed her. She missed the laughs she and her mum had had. The easy companionable afternoons just chatting or watching television or wandering around a garden centre.

Janey's children missed their grandparents too. It seemed hard sometimes, Janey thought, to be the head of the family. All three of her very well-meaning children had encouraged her to get a puppy at various times. Even before her Gizmo had died, so that she wouldn't be without a dog. Their motives were all well intentioned. But things were different for Janey now. Her whole world had changed in all sorts of subtle and not so subtle ways over the last few years and getting another dog was not in her future plans. She felt the time was right for her to have some time for herself. For the first time ever it seemed that she'd be able to put her desires into action. She felt a bit guilty and a little selfish planning to do her own thing but she pushed such thoughts to the back of her mind. She'd spent a long time putting others first and now it was her time. If only she could make up her mind exactly what to do and how she'd manage to afford it.

Chapter 3

Fraser kept waving until he turned the corner. He'd always done it. Whether going to school, the shops, work and now just off to see his pals, he knew his wave meant a lot to his mum. Well, OK, it meant a lot to him too. Christ, it was sad about the dog. Fraser was really cut up about it. Seventeen years of his life. His wee pal. He wandered up their road in the comfortable area of Craiglockhart in Edinburgh, head down, fighting the tears. Past the cherry tree that always seemed to have a branch fallen down but never got smaller. Past the post box that he used to drop his mum's letters into when he was wee and be thrilled when she trusted him to do it alone. Past the wall that he and his siblings used to walk along much to the annoyance of the homeowner who'd chase them if they got caught. It made it all the more exciting and made them all the more determined to do it. Fraser still remembered the time his sister Iona dared them to jump off the highest end. He'd been fine but Donald had fallen awkwardly and protested about the pain in his wrist all afternoon so that they all had to confess to mucking about. It had been so boring at the Sick Kid's Hospital later that evening and Don had got all the attention. Looking at the wall, Fraser realised it wasn't as tall as it was when he was younger. I must be growing up, he thought. That would be a first – quite a scary one too. He was looking forward to going back to University in a few weeks' time, the summer holidays were long and he missed the socialising. Meanwhile he worked at the same boring supermarket as his mum. It was tedious but gave him some cash to go out with his friends. He had been trying to persuade his mum to quit. Fraser knew that hundreds of years ago his mum had been to university and trained as a nurse. Consequently it frustrated him that she stayed at the supermarket, even if it was convenient, especially as the new manager was a real bully. All the staff just kept their heads down, got on with their jobs and sooked up to her. She loved to wax lyrical to anyone who visited about the "closeness of the team" and how the working atmosphere was wonderful. Then she'd be a complete bitch to one of the staff. Fraser reckoned the senior manager was the only one who couldn't see how her two-faced attitude lowered staff morale. No wonder her nickname was "Cruella De Ville".

Tonight was going to be good. He lifted his head as he walked and took a deep breath. He'd keep his tears for another time and put on his cheery face. Maybe his sadness at his dog dying would soften the heart of the girl he fancied.

He did worry about his mum though. She'd always been there for all of them and now she was going to be on her own. He wanted to move out like his brother and sister, but he had a fierce loyalty to his mum, maybe because he was the youngest. And of course it was cheaper. He passed the big house at the corner and looked to see if his bus was coming. Nothing yet. He reached the bus stop. The traffic was much busier on the main road. Their wee house was tucked away in a sleepy corner close to the park. He ran his fingers through his hair. He quite liked his blond hair, which was always a talking point with the girls, being long and straight. He had a notion to dye it dark to match his dark eyebrows, but his mum would probably have a fit. And he should really tidy his room; that would cheer her up. She was always moaning about the state of it. He just couldn't be bothered taking glasses and dishes downstairs and they seemed to multiply all by themselves so that she'd complain about running out of stuff. Maybe he'd tidy up tomorrow.

As he waited for the bus, he thought about the gig he was going to. His mates were playing tonight. Fraser wished he had the guts to play in public; he loved his guitar. Once he was back at uni he'd think about joining a band. Probably a debating society would be more him, he thought, or a drama group. He'd loved drama at school and now that he was doing history he'd have the chance to do other things as well. Fraser had always liked everything to do with history. He and his mum had probably visited all the castles in Scotland and he loved the highlands. And many "piles of rubble" as he'd called them when he was wee. His favourite place in the entire world was Culloden Battlefield in the north of Scotland, near Inverness. He made a promise to himself to visit soon especially now that the new visitor centre was open. He looked up at the trees and saw that the leaves were all turning. Maybe his mum was right? Maybe a new dog wasn't the solution?

The bus rumbled slowly up to the stop. Typical thought Fraser, just when I need to be on time – a slow bloody bus. He hoped the young lady he had his eye on would still be there. With the pleasant feelings those thoughts brought, he hopped on.

Chapter 4

Fraser wasn't the only one waiting for a bus in Edinburgh that night.

His mum's man-hungry friend, Katie, had been late night shopping and was exhausted. She worked in a printer's as a graphic designer. The job was good and paid well. They had a decent set of clients but every job meant deadlines. They'd just finished a big order for wedding stationery. The bride had been fine, but her mother was a nightmare. It took Katie back to her own wedding – not a thought she relished nowadays, and how interfering her own mother had been.

She'd married young at twenty and the wedding planning had been a nightmare. The mothers had handled all the organisation, she'd hardly had a say in anything. Carried away so much, she'd been quite unable to voice her doubts as the day drew nearer. 'Wedding nerves' everyone had said. And her friend Janey had been just as bad. Married only nine months earlier, she'd been in the honeymoon period. God, how that had changed.

Katie felt really sorry for Janey. She'd done the right thing, eventually, and horsed that no mark of a husband out. Not that anyone had realised just quite what a controlling bastard he'd been until he'd left. It came as a shock when Janey finally confided in her one night after their badminton club had been out for an end of year drink.

Janey had been the designated driver, as usual, and had dropped Katie off last. When she'd asked Janey why she always drove, she'd been shocked into sobriety when her friend dissolved into tears as she clutched the steering wheel. It had all come tumbling out and they'd sat for ages outside Katie's house. How Janey had had another row with

Nick. That the rows were getting longer and more violent, both physical and emotional and that she couldn't stand much more of it. Katie was horrified; everyone thought Janey had the perfect marriage, three lovely kids and a husband that adored her. Katie had always been very open about her own pain in the neck, Tim. Their fall-outs were legendary and a great source of mirth on nights out. Funny after the event. Katie wondered if Janey had ever laughed about her past. She certainly never talked about it now.

The night of the badminton night out, Nick had forbidden Janey to go, but she'd stood her ground. She'd showed Katie the clear finger marks on her arm, which were already threatening to be a cracking bruise.

Thank God that was behind her now, Katie thought. She'd have to find a way to convince Janey to come on their next girly weekend. Katie peeked into the bag with the new hiking boots she'd bought that evening. She'd found the perfect place for their next weekend trip, a retreat up near Inverness in the highlands called Aigas. The crowd that went on their trips were both friends from their childhood and new friends; everyone was welcome, although there was rarely more than six of them at a time. Not everyone could get away what with work and family commitments.

Katie was a real bookish person and just loved the Edinburgh International Book Festival every August. She spent a fortune on books that lasted her the whole year. She and Janey shared a passion for reading. They'd always talked about joining a book club, but preferred to swap amongst themselves.

Katie had been at the talk by Sir John Lister-Kaye about his book, *Song of The Rolling Earth*. She'd been entranced with the story of how he and his wife, Lucy had bought the crumbling Victorian hunting lodge, Aigas, and brought it to life as a world-renowned naturalist centre now visited by hundreds each year interested in birdlife, the environment, the countryside and even the re-introduction of beavers.

It would be a beautiful place for a walking weekend with good company, evenings of cosy drinks and laughter.

On a lighter note, Katie wished someone would take note of her beaver. It seemed a long time since she'd enjoyed anything other than a passing fling. That was another thing she and Janey should do – find themselves a couple of decent men. If there were any left, she thought. What had happened to all the good, considerate, kind, sensitive, good-looking men? Oh, yes, she remembered the old punch line – they all had boyfriends.

The bus queue was long and the bus well overdue. Katie was tired after her busy workday and then fighting through all the shoppers in town. That chilled Pinot Grigio was languishing in her fridge at home, but not for long she hoped. She should call Janey and get her over for a glass or two. She rarely said 'yes' though. Happy in her own wee world was Janey: kids, her dog, and her crappy job. And she'd really let herself go.

Not like Katie who prided herself on her good looks and figure, despite three kids. The same as Janey, but she'd gained weight after all of them that she'd never bothered to shift. And she used to be so sporty, Katie remembered.

Katie wouldn't be seen dead outside without make-up. She'd even do her face if she was popping round to the supermarket. And although a red-head in her youth, she used just the right shade of blond on her hair to pass as quite natural. And it was always styled into a long bob, framing her face. Katie wondered if maybe Janey was a bit jealous of her post-divorce glamour. And Katie was a slave to the calorie counting. Janey used to tease her about the encyclopaedic knowledge Katie had of the number of calories in any food. Katie only counted the calories in food though, never in the wine.

Janey never complained, but Katie could see she was definitely getting bored with her life, especially now that the kids were almost all gone.

The bus came and, as Katie sank down gratefully in a seat, she decided to take Janey in hand and sort them both out. She'd give her a call and then get the others to help when they went on their night out. And the Girly Weekend was the perfect start.

Chapter 5

Janey was 'mirror moaning'. She was getting ready for yet another shift at the supermarket. She'd pick up something for her tea on her break. No Fraser to feed tonight. Then she'd settle for some telly and curl up with a book. An avid reader, Janey loved the feeling of being transported to another place. Fiction was her favourite but, encouraged by Katie's passion for all books she'd discovered some great biographies and travel books.

Peter Kerr's books about his life in Majorca, buying an orange grove and the hilarious stories about him and his family trying to make a go of living there were amongst her favourites. She'd love to go to Majorca and visit some of the places he wrote about.

So here she was in her magnolia bedroom, the only splash of colour the patchwork quilt she'd made years earlier from fabric she'd used to make clothes for the kids when they were small. Offcuts of the different phases of her life. All different, coming together to make a very special quilt. Maybe she should be thankful that although getting a bit boring, her life was more together now than it had ever been.

Janey seldom contemplated herself in a mirror. She wondered what others saw when they looked at her. In general she disliked the fact than mirrors no longer reflected back the good-looking twenty-something she'd once been. She was in her late forties and a bit overweight. No, she was a lot overweight really, but as she had been fit and active in her youth it meant she usually fooled herself into thinking that only a small effort would bring back her slender figure. Who was she fooling – her wine waist simply refused to be concealed in anything less than a size eighteen. She often thought she was going to end up a slave to the stretch waist trousers so favoured by her elderly mother.

At only five foot two it just wasn't a good look. She was proud of her long, dark wavy hair but all too often it was scraped back in a bun to keep the curls from escaping. That's how it was today. She wished she had the courage to get it chopped off and be sleek and made up like Katie. Her hair was also a bit grey – not that you'd notice thanks to chemical help – she hid it well, just like all her pals. Not one of them had given in to the grey yet – just give it time.

Yes, Janey had to admit – she was fat. And it was about time she did something about it. Even the dog had betrayed her. He'd not needed the long walks of his youth and just before he died a slow stroll to the end of the road was all he wanted. After many years as a dog owner, Janey felt a bit bonkers walking without a dog in tow. She was very, very bored with her job, and very, very divorced. That last fact wasn't bad, she'd been divorced for so long, she often forgot her ex even existed. The children had got birthday and Christmas cheques until a certain age, but he had never been the keeping in touch type of father.

He'd been fairly good when they were together and the kids were little as long as Janey did all that was expected of her, organised the children, school, holidays, household bills, dinner at night and made him look like the best dad in the world.

Then, eventually she woke up and smelled the coffee.

Thank goodness she would never have to put up with his secret bullying ways again. What a shock it had been to the world when he left – he'd seemed such a paragon to their friends and family. Not everything was as it seemed to the outside world.

Not having to think about her in-laws was a huge advantage to being divorced. Never to have her snobby mother-in-law to deal with. She'd even given up on her grandchildren – her perfect son had clearly been hard done by and Janey knew she'd never be forgiven.

Her loss, not mine, Janey thought.

Parts of Edinburgh could be incredibly snobby – keeping nasty things hidden, not talking about personal stuff. It was full of "twtichers", nosey (generally old but some not so old like her ex mother-in law) women peeking out from behind the curtains gathering gossip that did no one any good.

But you were expected to keep smiling, whatever happened.

Even her own mother had been in the 'YMYB' brigade – 'You've Made Your Bed (so lie in it)' – until the whole story had come out. Janey wished she'd been able to confide in her mum a lot earlier.

Nick had been far too selfish for family life and too wrapped up in himself – but of course now he had his new family – and let's face it, Janey laughed, who would want twins at fifty? That was divine retribution if ever I saw it, thought Janey with a smug grin.

Then she felt immediately guilty, his new wife was really nice and in the short time she and the kids had been allowed to be in contact with her, she'd been lovely. Much younger, but then that's what Nick had said as she threw him out,

"I'll get a younger blonde one next – and an only child as well so I'll have some money." And he did just that.

The best thing she'd done was to get rid of him, and she recalled glowing with pride at the "Well Done" cards her girlfriends had sent. Janey had quite a party when the divorce came through and all her best buddies and most supportive friends came over to the house. And there was Katie, of course. Katie had organised the party, she understood how Janey felt. Katie was trapped in a difficult marriage as well, then. She'd eventually got out of it and now Janey was very grateful for her friendship.

Instead of feeling a failure, Katie and the others made her feel that she had achieved something really significant.

Janey felt she was coming to a big turning point in her life. And she knew she had to make some changes before her courage ran out and she ended up sticking to her familiar, safe routine.

She had been a conformer in her younger days. Her dad had had high hopes for her. University and a glittering career. Janey hadn't fancied that. She'd trained as a nurse at Queen Margaret College in Edinburgh instead. And stayed at home throughout.

She sometimes thought she'd only got married to leave home. And although she hadn't worked for long after she got married, she'd loved nursing. But marriage at twenty and a baby eighteen months later had turned her into a meek housewife. She'd loved being a mum and had thrown herself into motherhood. Even post-natal depression after Iona hadn't put her off having another. And thank goodness for them now. She'd been young enough to grow up with them and had had the energy to cope with them all. And now Janey was hoping she had enough energy to have some fun for herself. She'd been no nun since she and Nick divorced, but nothing special had happened in the love department, so she settled for her own company more and more. That would have to change too.

Janey's friend, Katie had got married not long after Janey. After the divorce Katie had even commented about Janey's pioneering antics: first to get married; first to have children; first to get divorced.

"And about bloody time too." had been Katie's reaction when she called her once Nick had left. Katie had rushed over and given her a big girlie hug and held Janey until she crumpled in tears.

"Oh god, Katie, I don't know what to tell the kids, they'll blame me for getting rid of their dad."

"Don't be daft, Janey, after Nick's latest outburst, they'll be glad of the peace in the house. They've been scared for a long time, and probably protecting you. They may be young, and all under ten, but they're not stupid. They've seen him having a go at you now. They've heard the shouting and their wee imaginations will be running riot. I'll stay with you and help you tell them."

"But what if they blame me forever. I couldn't cope with them hating me for all of this."

"They won't, just be as honest as you can and remember, they're young. You're a good mum and they love you. It'll be really tough at first but you'll get through. I just wish I had the courage to get rid of Tim."

And Katie had been right. It had been tough but they'd all worked as a family team and with the support of her friends and her parents, Janey had turned it around. Janey didn't think of herself as pioneering, just the opposite, but her confidence had grown after her divorce, and she felt all the better for it. Her kids were great and included her in a lot in what they did and she got out to see her friends regularly, which saved her sanity, there was nothing like a group of women out for a blether to get a true perspective on life. Women were amazing like that – even women you hardly knew, maybe a friend of a friend that had come out for the evening and after five minutes you could swap life stories and be like best mates.

Janey had a good group of friends. Some, like Katie, she'd known for a long time. Others were friends she'd met through the children. School gate mums like herself. And some that she'd met through groups she'd belonged to, like the badminton group. She'd stopped going a long time ago but still met up with a few of the girls. Janey was sure she'd never fit into her badminton skirt again. That was another challenge she'd have to tackle sooner or later.

Janey pulled on her coat and headed off to work. She just wished something would happen to get her out of the rut she was in. Losing the dog seemed like another blow. Pull yourself together, she chided herself, look on the bright side, maybe it's time for new beginnings. She wished that something would happen.

Then the voice of her dad popped into her head, what was it he used to say? Ah yes, "Be careful of what you wish for."

I'll just have to wish for good things, she thought. Maybe a bit of positive thinking was required. And there was the night out to look forward to, just two days left.

She pulled back her shoulders as she walked up the road. Maybe 'Cruella De Ville' would be off today. Now that was a good wish.

Chapter 6

At last it was the weekend. Janey sighed with pleasure as she came up the path. With any luck the warm autumn weather would hold and she'd be able to tidy the garden. She absentmindedly bent down and picked a weed from between the paving stones in the path. She might even be able to get an hour of much needed gardening in this evening. The garden wasn't big at the front but Janey always thought the front should be welcoming and neat. A bit like herself really. Maybe she should go mad and have a wild front garden. Turn all bohemian. She laughed to herself. What would folk say? "Good old (not SO old) Janey's gone mad now that she's heading for fifty." She looked in her bag for her keys. It didn't really matter which bag she had with her, however big or small, she could never find her keys. What was it about handbags? Even when she tried to discipline herself to always use the same pocket, the key fairies always moved them.

She put her key into the main lock but the door swung open. Janey was cautious, Fraser wasn't expected home yet. He usually went to watch the boys play in their band on a Friday and the first she'd hear of him was bumbling in at three in the morning if at all. A cheery "Hi mum." dispelled the rush of panic. Fraser was spread on the couch surrounded by sweetie wrappers and a bottle of Irn Bru.

"I thought you'd be out." Janey was glad to see him though.

"Great to see you too."

"I just thought you'd be away watching Rory's band"

"They're not on till later so I thought I'd come back and catch a shower. I've ordered pizza If you want some. Pepperoni."

"I might just do that. Thanks for the offer."

Janey knew if she had any chance of a slice of pizza she'd have to catch the delivery man on the path. Then she remembered her promise to herself.

"No pizza for me, thanks love, I'm counting my calories." God, I sound like Katie, Janey laughed at herself.

Then Fraser burst in to laughter, "You, Mum, why?"

"Because, in case you hadn't noticed, I'm too fat."

"No, you're not, you're my cuddly mum."

"Well, I can still be cuddly, just less of me," Janey was laughing too.

"You're not getting anorexic just because the dog's died, are you?" Fraser feigned shock.

"Hardly, just wanting to look better in the store uniform. And maybe stop the hints from Cruella De Ville. God that woman annoys me. She reckons all women over forty should have short hair and that we should all be obsessed by our weight."

"Hey, it was a joke – you go for it, Ma, I like the way you're beginning to stand up for yourself at work. It's about time someone sorted her out. Funny how she never picks on us blokes."

"Oh, no, she likes to be popular with the boys."

Janey was still laughing as she put her shopping away.

One of Janey's friends at work had given her a crash course in dieting, when she'd plucked up the courage to ask.

"Don't do any of these faddy ones," offered Rosemary, "They just make you put weight on all the faster when you stop. Just look for the calories in everything and give yourself a limit."

"But I haven't a clue," groaned Janey as she sat with her cup of tea and a muffin during their break.

"Well that muffin for a start. You could eat a whole meal for the calories in that."

"I really am going to have to cut right down. I suppose all the comfort treats have to go."

"Och, you can allow yourself the odd treat. Just not every day. It's a bit like finding a good balanced diet that you enjoy.

About changing habits. The most successful diets are the ones you never have to give up. It all just becomes a way of life."

Rosemary had been following the same guidelines for a while now and had lost quite a bit of weight. "And exercise of course. I go to a great gym in Morningside so it's not that far away. It's called "The Club". The staff are really helpful and one of the trainers, Roxy – I'm sure that's not her real name, fairly puts me though my paces. She's a hoot, huge personality, Barbie Doll figure - no, really, I'm sure she only ever eats raw veg. But she's so warm and encouraging it's a real pleasure to go there. She's one of the owners too, so you get really special treatment. You should give it a try. They even give discounts for single parents…" Rosemary tailed off, blushing. Rosemary was renowned for putting her foot in it. Janey was such a private person, but although Rosemary hadn't gone too far, Janey noticed her embarrassment, but was glad of the other woman's help. Janey was always the shoulder for everyone to lean on; it felt strange to Janey that she should be taking more of an interest in herself. Janey smiled.

"That is helpful, Rosemary. I'm fed up of looking in the mirror and not seeing the slim young thing I used to be. Not that I'd ever be THAT slim again," Janey chuckled, "But at least I might find a waist. I hate exercising being this shape, but if I'm going to be in a bikini this time next year, I'd better start now."

"Going somewhere nice? I didn't realise you were going abroad next year. It's usually Skye, isn't it? Unless global warming means there's more chance of wearing a bikini than a cagoule."

"I'm off to Majorca." The words were out before Janey had even thought about them. Where exactly had that statement come from? She hadn't even considered going abroad up until that point. Clearly her hormones were getting the better of her. She was clearly having a menopausal moment and talking drivel.

"But that's fantastic, we were in Puerto Pollensa last year and it was lovely. You'll have a great time. Even on your own."

Janey didn't comment. She'd shocked herself by putting her wishes into words. Maybe she'd just have to go now. It would give her a year to save and a year to get fitter and slimmer. A bubble of real pleasure started deep down and she gave Rosemary a smile of genuine happiness.

"Let me have the details of the club and I'll sign up with Roxy on Monday."

Janey recounted the conversation with Rosemary to Fraser as he munched his pizza. But she left out the bit about Majorca. He would think she'd flipped entirely. One bit at a time for the kids. The change would be gradual.

"Good on you, Mum. About time you did something for yourself. Find out how old this Roxy is and I might join up with you." Boys and their one-track minds, smiled Janey. She took herself off to the kitchen to fix a suitably low calorie tea. The choccy biccies would have to wait. Wait until she told the girls tomorrow night that she was on a diet. No, not a diet, just eating healthily.

She took out the details Rosemary had given her about the club and called. A lovely young man, at least he sounded young, put her immediately at her ease and even suggested a 'no strings attached' visit. She discovered they'd even give advice on diet and had a visiting masseur and a Reiki therapist. Janey had always fancied giving Reiki a try. The idea of that total relaxation appealed. It would be another new experience to add to her list. There was no waiting list at The Club, and before Janey realised she was booked in for an assessment visit the next day, why wait for Monday.

She seriously thought about doing a few sit-ups for practice's sake, then changed her mind and did her usual, tea with milk and sugar and two biscuits. That would keep her going until dinner. The diet could wait until tomorrow.

Chapter 7

The crowd of women that Janey met with occasionally was really quite big. There were her friends and friends of friends who'd joined in the group. They all got on really well, catching up on all the gossip. Someone would take the initiative, set a date for a girly night and as many of them as possible would meet for a drink and a blether. They were quite a motley crew all from different backgrounds. But with the common bond of getting on well, having fun, and enjoying escaping for a drink now and again. And there was even the annual girly weekend away.

There was Sally; 'Singing and Dancing Sally' they called her, she performed with a local drama group to make up for the rigidly boring job of working for the world's dullest and in her words "wankerish" lawyer. Luckily, he was so intimidated by her she got her own way when it came to flexitime and doctors' appointments for 'women's things' which he was far too scared to question.

Hilary was the teacher type. Not too conventional a teacher though, and as scatty as a fruitcake but with a heart of gold. She'd never forget a gift for Christmas or birthdays, it could just be six months late, but she had the most amazing personality that lit up any room she walked into. And Hilary was always at least an hour late for anything social.

Natalie had a high-powered job in finance, but could drink them all under the table. She didn't need to worry about a hangover, she'd no kids, just cute cats – which she'd argue *were* her children.

And the very classy Angela, also married with no children, and never a hair out of place. She was a size zero, but still insisted her hips were too big. Beside her, Janey felt like a happy hippo, a pigmy one of course. But Angela was a good friend even although she had an enviable aversion to food. But what they all had in common was the desire to escape into that heady world of girlie nonsense. They'd been meeting up for several years and had gone through all the ups and downs of life together. They were all older now with family/work/relationship commitments, so although the nights were always good fun, they weren't as wild as they used to be. As they all got older, so the reckless days were behind them.

Then there was Katie. Janey had known Hilary and Katie since they were all ten years old. When Katie got married they'd warned Katie that it would never last. And it didn't. But it took twenty-five years for her to escape. She and Janey were the only ones of their teenage crowd that had done the "get married and have kids" thing at an early age.

Katie had thrown a surprise twenty-fifth anniversary party for Tim (incredibly dim), her husband. He'd led her a merry dance all through their marriage. Janey and Katie had often talked about the trap they felt they were in. Janey had been able to escape years earlier but Katie was still hanging in. She'd kept the anniversary party secret well. Janey and Hilary had been there to offer moral support and marvel that despite the most tempestuous relationship, Katie and Tim had almost made it to their silver wedding. The party was planned to be a week early to avoid any suspicions from Tim. Katie's hardest job was keeping him sober enough to arrive at the Orwell Lodge Hotel near where they all lived. This she managed under the pretext of a charity function. She'd taken the sensible step of letting their children in on the secret and of the contents of her speech. Luckily, she had the backing of them all. Tim was extremely shocked to see all their family and friends there and immediately puffed out his chest and gave a splendid speech about his lovely wife and the special years they'd had together.

Katie was not so complimentary – her offering went along the lines of,

"I've invited you all here to this party so that I don't have to call you all individually. Thank you for all the support I've had over the last twenty-five years, most of you were quite right about me and Tim, over and over again, and now it's my turn to be right.

Tim, most of your belongings are in the hotel, here, and I've booked you in for a week. We're done. It's over for us."

There was total silence in the room. Katie savoured the moment and looked triumphantly round the room.

Tim's friends were genuinely shocked. Katie's friends just wanted to shout "Hallelujah!" By this time most of those in the room didn't really know what was going on but even those at the bar stopped chatting because clearly something was about to happen.

"You can pick up the rest your stuff some other time. The joiner is at the house changing the locks, so don't come home. And by the way, the party's a week before our anniversary so that I never have to say we were married for twenty-five years.

Oh – and here are the divorce papers."

Janey had never seen Katie look so happy and triumphant. The room began to rumble, low murmuring at first then the bellow of a man scorned shook the room. Luckily Katie had warned a couple of her bulkier male friends and they restrained the more than absolutely livid Tim while Katie, Hilary and Janey made a fast exit in gales of champagne fuelled giggles. Not wishing to waste time, they'd ordered a cab and went straight to the newly re-locked Katie's house, kicked off their shoes and danced the rest of the night away to *Status Quo*, *The Beatles* and *Shania Twain* amongst others. The next morning, Janey dimly remembered a bit of *Patsy Cline* and other power ballads in there too. Anything in fact that you could sing to holding a candlestick for a makeshift microphone, their trademark for a good girlie night out.

It hardly seemed like seven years had gone by.

In the months that followed it just became messy for Katie. But she was recovering well in her three bedroomed flat in Ravelston. Another 'Twitchers paradise', but Katie, like Janey, had adjusted eventually to the fact than now she could run her own life and what the gossips thought had little bearing on her. The girls in Janey's social group were all different. One or two were still married but it was alarming how many had taken the plunge into singledom. They all still met when they could, but what with work, babysitting, grumpy husbands etc., it was often really difficult. To try to get around this, the girls tried to organise an annual weekend away. Janie hadn't been on one for years, well, at least three. The last time it had been to some remote place and included lots of walking and fresh air, something Janey hadn't done since her student days. She'd even been into hill-walking and the outdoors, but the motherhood years had put paid to that. She'd even been quite a good skier in her time up at Hillend, the artificial ski-slope just outside Edinburgh, and occasionally venturing up north to Aviemore and Glenshee. She couldn't quite see herself hurtling down any hillsides nowadays. There simply wasn't a sexy snowsuit made for a dumpy five foot something.

Chapter 8

The weather had held, and Janey had been in the back garden most of the Saturday. Her back ached but she hoped the hours of weeding, pruning and cutting the grass had helped her shed a couple of pounds. She'd been for her first assessment at The Club that morning and had signed up for regular training from Roxy. Roxy was amazing and passionate about her work. She'd been so positive that even Janey was sure she'd be able to get fit again.

She had really enjoyed the session. The club wasn't too big so there was lots of personal attention, and Roxy was great fun. "You've got "muscle memory," Roxy had told her. "Whenever someone has been sporty in their teens, their muscles remember, so getting toned is much easier."

"Mine must have a bloody long memory then," Janey had puffed as she did another set of crunches.

Roxy had laughed, "Muscles are like elephants, they never forget."

"I feel like the size of an elephant." Janey had been quite despondent at first, but as the session went by, she felt like she was making a really positive start. All good. Janey had even been able to share her worries with Roxy about how she felt about herself and how much it had affected her confidence.

"You seem a well-grounded woman, Janey. I think as time goes on your confidence will grow and you'll feel better about yourself outside and inside. We'll soon be celebrating the emergence of a far stronger woman ready to face any challenge."

Janey was secretly thrilled about Roxy's positive outlook and warm, friendly but determined approach. She would become a friend as well as a trainer, Janey was sure.

Janey emerged from the memory and wiped the back of her hand over her brow and looked around. The apples were picked from the tree. It was a miniature variety she'd bought several years earlier on a garden centre trip with Katie. That's why she'd bought it; 'Katy' was the variety of apple it produced. They'd laughed at the time wondering if it was better to have a rose named after you or an apple. Janey crunched into the fresh sweet fruit. She could eat any number of apples and loved the other fruit her little patch grew. The gooseberries had been good this year, sweet dark red ones and made great jam. Janey would have to restrict herself to much smaller helpings from now on. The big cherry tree at the end of the garden was beginning to shed its leaves. The colours were glorious, reds, oranges and yellow. She recalled the children gathering them up and making pictures with leaves, glue and paint. Janey wondered vaguely as she looked round at her much tidier garden if other mothers had these random thoughts when places or objects or even smells brought back long forgotten memories. Anyhow, she thought she'd better get herself into the shower. It was the girl's night out and she was looking forward to it.

Fraser emerged from his room as she came into the house. "You should have been out in the garden, enjoying the sunshine." She sometimes thought Fraser was nocturnal, the hours he kept.

"I'm doing an extra shift at the supermarket tonight so needed my beauty sleep."

"What, twenty four hours, you must think you're ugly." Janey enjoyed the easy banter she and Fraser had. She would miss him when he moved out.

"SO funny. At least I'm not covered in dead leaves and things with a camouflage streak across my face."

One glance in the mirror and Janey was laughing too. "I'd better change this war paint before I go out. I won't get into the pub looking like this." she wiped at the smudge across her forehead. "Remember your keys, I'll be out when you get back." she called over her shoulder as she walked towards the bathroom.

"A hot date I hope?" quipped Fraser. He checked his hair, adjusted his jacket and headed for the door.

"No, just the girls."

"Ah, the Witches of Eastwick and the coven meeting." Fraser was out of the door and down the path before she could laughingly remonstrate.

Easing into the bath, the lavender bubbles felt glorious as Janey wallowed in the scent. She loved the feeling of the warm water on her skin and could feel the strained muscles relax as she gently soaped herself. Water was so sensual, the weightlessness making Janey feel better by the minute. Maybe she'd have to give up her solo sex life sometime soon. Water always had that effect on her. And swimming was the most sensual of all. Maybe once she'd lost a few pounds lost she'd venture into the local pool again. The trouble was after a swim she felt so refreshed and sexy, it made her single status all the more acute. She thought about the coming evening. She'd tell the girls about the healthy eating, but would leave out her plans for the holiday. She was anxious in case one of them might suggest coming with her. Since blurting out her until then unknown plans to Rosemary, the thought had grown. And she had come round to liking the idea of travelling alone. So she'd keep her plans secret for now. She left her soothing bath reluctantly and headed for the bedroom. The towel was soft and comforting but she resisted the temptation to put on her PJ's and sorted out something to wear.

The late, low sun streamed into her room, she loved this time of day and this season, and then she turned her attention to transforming the plain Jane to the happy socialising Janey.

The plan was they'd meet in Giuliano's Restaurant in the town centre, and then decide where to go after that. Giuliano's was a warm, friendly Italian restaurant that Janey knew well because her friend, Sally, had worked there many years ago as a waitress. Everyone was friendly there, the owners and the staff and the food was excellent. They knew the girly nights would be a lot of fun and they always gave them a good table (usually where they couldn't disturb the other diners with their laughter). Often, after the meal, the blethering would take over and they'd settle there for the whole evening. Gone were the days of "The Challenge".

The challenge was that they'd all have enough money in their purses for the taxi home. That was the rule. The other rule was staying together. Safety in numbers. Then it would be a competition to see who could get the most drinks bought for them in the evening – by guys of course – with an emergency tenner for the fainthearted. They must have seemed like a complete troop of predators. She had to admit, though, they'd had some laughs at the time. Especially when they'd ended up in The Cavendish for a dance. It was in the Tollcross area of Edinburgh and the place where safety in numbers really counted. The trick at The Cavendish, or 'The Cav' as it was known locally, was never to let the numbers drop below four women otherwise the predatory male species would move in for unwelcome offers to dance. Those were real 'dancing round your handbag' nights.

Janey was looking forward to reminding some of the girls about their young and reckless ways. Maybe she was feeling a little like that now. She had life-changing plans forming in her mind. They'd all think she was barking mad but she didn't care. She'd be the first to have her midlife crisis. It wasn't reckless nights out nowadays, the girly chat and bar supper always seemed to be enough. They met so infrequently and there was so much to catch up on that the gossip seemed to take over. Janey was looking forward to the evening.

Janey put the finishing touches to her make-up. She looked at herself in the mirror. Quite a pretty face, when she remembered to smile. Good legs too, only she always hid them in trousers. Trousers were much more comfortable than skirts and hid a multitude of sins, especially black trousers. It was amazing how many of the girlies turned up in black trousers. Well, at least they all had the same hang-ups.

Her top was lovely though, a wee bit of cleavage showing; if you've got it, flaunt it; and just the right amount of sparkles scattered amongst the soft red lambs' wool. And she loved the three-quarter sleeves this time of year. With the extra fluffy scarf and black (of course) jacket, she was ready to go. The taxi would be here soon having already picked up two of the girls first.

She checked the empty house, locked up, missed the goodbye to her beloved doggie, wondered what manner of less than sober student types she'd find lounging about when she got home and hurried to the waiting taxi. She had a funny feeling that this was going to be a really good night.

Chapter 9

Janey felt so very lucky. A great night out with them getting more outrageous as the wine flowed was pretty much on the cards. The noise from their table was full of laughter. Giuliano was the perfect host along with all the other staff. They'd started the evening with a glass of prosecco.

"Here's to good friends, great food and lots of wine." They all raised their glasses as Hilary made the first toast of the evening.

"Here's to new beginnings and perhaps some romance for those of us left on the shelf."

"Romance? You don't want romance, just great sex." Sally could always be relied upon to bring a smile to their faces.

Janey interrupted, "I'd love a bit of romance thank you. There must still be some decent men left, surely? Men that want more than just sex. What about love, companionship and having fun together? You know, walking hand in hand into the sunset?"

"I don't know how you stay so positive Janey. After all you've been through and you still believe in the Knight in Shining Armour riding on his white charger to sweep you off your feet. Life just isn't like that; all the good men are taken by this age. Just saying. Neither of us has been very lucky in our choice of life partners."

"Don't be so gloomy, Katie. Just because we've chosen badly in the past, doesn't mean we can't love again. I don't know about you, but the one thing my marriage taught me is that men like my ex are wired up in a different way from most men, we were just unlucky. My next committed relationship will be far more equal. I will not be trampled on again."

"So how do you work out which is which?" Katie drained her glass and called the waiter over to see the wine list.

"Red, white or rosé ladies?"

"You know the answer to that Scott, it's the same as usual. One of each to start and then on to limoncello all round I think. Is that right girls?" Sally looked around the table.

"Only one of each, ladies? Have you taken the pledge?" Scott laughed at the table of women.

"No need to be greedy for now, but I think you know us so well." Sally stood up and gave him a big hug. "I don't suppose you've got any good-looking brothers hidden away, keen to meet the likes of us?"

"If I did, I'd be warning them first," Scott took their banter in his stride and walked away laughing as he went to get the first of many bottles he knew they would get through that evening.

He'd probably come and join them as the customers left. The restaurant was very busy, but he always took the time to chat for a few minutes. That's what makes the place so popular Janey thought.

"Here's to those who couldn't join us tonight. They know what they're missing and perhaps be here next time," Janey raised her glass in a toast. "Now, down to business. Who's going on the girly weekend. Sadly, I can't this year, but I'll be with you in spirit and I'm sure you'll all fill me in with whatever fun you get up to."

"You should come Janey, you've not been for ages and it would do you good." Hilary hugged her friend, "It's always good fun when you come with us."

"Sorry Hilary, I just don't have the funds at the moment, and Christmas is coming up."

"Oh come on, your kids are all grown up now. It's time for you to put yourself first," Hilary replied.

"Exactly, let me see if I can tempt you," Katie said fishing out her mobile phone and sharing photos of the retreat. "That's the hunting lodge, and that's the world renowned naturalist centre."

"So, you expect us to get our kit off?" Sally was shocked.

"No, but I do expect you to come walking with me. Aigas is a centre for the study of nature, not a nudist camp."

Janey signed, "I'm sorry, I just can't afford it. Think of me in that bloody supermarket while you are away."

"You should go, Janey. I'm not able to go this time round and you should be there to keep an eye on the others, especially Katie." Sally put her head to one side and looked hopefully at Janey.

"What do you mean, especially me?"

"Well Katie, you'll have your radar homed to every single man in a twenty mile radius, and they'll want to bring you back in one piece."

"It may not be me looking for eligible men, Janey might be the one to stray, now that she's on her make-over mission."

"I have no intention of looking for a man at the moment, and anyway, I'd probably have far more choice in the city rather than in the highlands. But I just don't have the cash flow. So please all stop trying to brow beat me into submission, I'll hear all about it when you get back. Come on, we have wine to drink and good food to share. Anyone for a refill?" Janey held out the wine bottle.

"Well, I don't mind if I do." Katie held up her glass and the others followed. "More wine please Scott."

"So that's just Katie, Hilary, Natalie and me heading north? I'll sort out the picnic for the cars as Janey's staying behind. Shame, you do a better job than me Janey."

"Enough Angela, don't you join in the with the persuasion. Discussion closed."

"We'll miss you," Hillary added.

"Well I have enough on my plate at the moment and I do need to make changes. I'm thinking about getting another job. I can't stand the boss, she's a real bully, and although I really like the rest of the staff, she's making my life a misery."

Scott appeared with more wine, to cheers from the table. "Speak to Giuliano Janey, he'd give you a job here, now that would be fun."

"I love the idea Scott, but I really think I'm too old to be working evenings. I like pottering in the garden or just chilling in front of the TV."

"Well you're never going to find a man with evening habits like that." Angela chided, "Maybe a job here would help you find the knight you're looking for."

"Well, I might just think about that, you do have a point. Maybe a couple of evening shifts at the local pub would be a good thing. Get me out of my comfort zone. Here's to the future."

They all raised their newly filled glasses and tucked into their Italian banquet.

Chapter 10

Janey clambered out of the taxi, paid the driver and stumbled back into her house, briefly puzzled at the lack of woofing greeting before she hazily remembered why. The excess of fluffy wine, as her kids called sparkling wine, "Because it made their mum go all 'fluffy.'" And large gins with bitter lemon, brought stinging tears to her eyes as she realised there would be no more faithful companion greeting her with the same enthusiasm whatever state she returned home in. The hot, booze-fuelled tears were threatening to overwhelm her when she noticed the answering machine blinking. That was quite unusual; most folk called Fraser and her on their mobiles rather than the house phone.

Janey went over and pressed the flashing button. The call had come in at 11:06pm – also unusual. She checked her mobile but there were no missed calls. Now she was focussing much better at the thought that it might be bad news. It really had to be if someone was calling her that late on a Saturday night. She pressed playback.

Janey crumpled onto the floor. Shock and gin both kicking in. Her fuzzy head muddled her thoughts and she wished she had someone to talk to. But that wasn't possible, not at three o'clock in the morning. Even the dog was dead. He'd always been such a good listener. And clearly Fraser was still out. The kitchen was tidy; there was no music or the faint aroma of beer and cigarettes from his bedroom. Even though forbidden to smoke in the house and especially his room; when the beer pixies were out to play, Fraser was unable to resist the adolescent in him who thought it would be fine if he hung out of this window, as if no one would know.

Janey hauled herself up. The temptation to stay on all fours and simply crawl to the warmth of the lounge was overwhelming but there were limits to how embarrassing one could be, even when alone. So she stood shakily and made a squinty bee-line for the booze cabinet. She had a memory flash of a radio programme. They'd explained why it was called a 'bee-line'. Apparently because bees work out the shortest distance from flower to flower to conserve energy, hence, bee-line. Janey was clearly a boozy bee but managed to pour herself a large whisky – as though she needed it. But the news she'd heard on the answering machine was staggering.

It was a call from a lawyer. For once not about divorce or custody, Janey hadn't had to worry about those calls for a long time. No, rather this one was from her aunt's lawyer in Canada. Something of a pleasant change. It would have been mid-afternoon in Canada when the lawyer had called. Her strangely familiar North American accent had sounded so glamorous on the answering machine. Janey's aunt, the only close relative left on her dad's side, had died the previous week. She'd been in her nineties and very frail, the only person Janey ever wrote a real letter to now. On an air-mail letter form. Now she'd never use the new packet she'd bought only the other day form the post office. Her Aunt Bridie, from Irish, Catholic, Canadian stock had been married to Janey's Uncle Jack and lived in Calgary. Jack had died years ago. Bridie had been one of five sisters to emigrate to Canada from Ireland, the only one to marry, but she couldn't have any children. Now Bridie was the only sister left. Only she wasn't, Janey reminded herself, now even her aunt was gone. Two deaths within a couple of weeks. Janey wondered anxiously if there would be another one. Things happened in threes. Her mother would have told her to break a match to break the bad luck. Janey would, just in case. Not usually given to superstition, some childhood habits just stuck. Janey's granny was the most superstitious person she'd ever met. She had a saying for everything and some really odd ideas. Her granny even used to take the telephone off the hook and hide any cutlery during thunderstorms. Janey wasn't as bad as that, she thought reaching for a match.

Her Aunt Bridie had doted on Janey and had even paid for her to have a six week holiday when she was eleven, touring Canada with Bridie and her Uncle Jack. Her Aunt and Uncle thought Janey might get bored only being with them, so they had brought Chris, their thirteen-year-old next-door-neighbour with them. Chris was a couple of years older but they shared a passion for swimming and Janey still kept in touch with Chris although it was by e-mail now. They'd toured Canada, staying in motels or with friends of her Aunt and Uncle and had many adventures. Aunt Bridie had always been generous to Janey's children, remembering birthdays and Christmas. For the past few years, Aunt Bridie had been in a nursing home, but a very caring home and Janey had often spoken to the nurses. Janey tried to call every couple of months and had only spoken to her Aunt a few weeks ago. Although Bridie sounded frail, she still had her sense of humour. Janey hadn't expected her to go so quickly, although perhaps going peacefully in her sleep was a blessing. Now, like the dog, she was gone. And like all the others, family and animals, Janey wondered if the long arm of death would ever stop harassing her.

This arm, however, had a generous open hand. A hand that held a generous cheque. "Generous", the lawyer had said. There was nothing in the message to say how much. She'd always thought that all her aunt's money would have been used up for the nursing home, but clearly not. The kind lawyer hadn't wanted to leave a message on her answering machine, but she'd done so as she needed to talk to Janey as soon as possible in case she called the nursing home. She'd also been instructed not to let Janey know until after the funeral so that she wouldn't feel obliged to attend, and now Janey had a generous inheritance. The lawyer was going on holiday but her partner would sort out the paperwork and get in touch with Janey in a few days. She sat in the lounge curled up on the couch. She felt cold despite the warmth of the coal fire. Janey sat by the fading glow of the fire, thank goodness she'd topped it up before she'd gone out for the night, cradling her single malt whisky between her shaky hands. A huge sadness overwhelmed her and the hot tears previously shed for the dog, and now for a much loved aunt, became a steady flow. Janey was roused by Fraser easing the empty glass from her hand and carefully placing a blanket over her. She snuggled into the cushions on the couch and drifted back to the dreamless sleep that would allow her heart to start the long process of healing.

The new morning might herald a day of new beginnings and changing lives.

Chapter 11

The morning did indeed bring a change. And not just in the weather, which matched Janey's mood – dull and drizzly. Her head thumped, unaccustomed to the alcohol from the previous night. How old do you have to be, thought Janey, before sensible drinking habits apply?

She'd woken about five, realised she was still in the lounge, fully clothed, and had stumbled to her bedroom, thrown off her clothes and after another few hours sleep, the events that greeted her tipsy return home started to sink in.

She felt more waves of sadness, but was glad her aunt would be safe with her heavenly family and not in any more pain.

She got up, reluctantly, removed last night's make-up – a sure sign that far too much booze had been consumed – managed a shower, a large glass of orange juice and a paracetamol. The dull ache in her head finally began to subside.

She called the number that had been left on the answer machine, unsure if there would be any response at the weekend. But as it turned out the call was answered and an hour later she knew the full story and the consequences to herself.

She ended the call and made herself a large cup of tea. She really should cut down on the sugar and milk, but not now.

She was rich. Not in a millionaire sort of way, but she'd have enough to stop working at the supermarket. She could take time to decide what she really wanted to do in the future. Janey couldn't imagine never working again, but she knew she should find something she really wanted to do. And maybe take a holiday. Majorca. She sat at the kitchen table cradling her tea and with that positive thought; the sun struggled through and brightened the kitchen and also her mood.

Janey hadn't thought what she was going to do with the money. The lawyer had talked vaguely about investing the money to give her a steady income, but Janey knew nothing about that sort of thing. She'd advised her to keep the money in high interest account at the bank and take advice from an advisor. An "Independent Financial Advisor" she'd warned.

"Go to a bank or building society and they can only advise you on their own products (a new term for Janey) whereas an Independent Advisor is just that. I can't advise because the rules are all different in every country. And anyway, I'm a lawyer, I know nothing about investing money."

So much was whirling around her head – new horizons would open up to her now. She'd go for her girly weekend and maybe find the space amongst the glorious scenery of The Highlands to really think about which direction her life should go in.

Janey felt at a real crossroads. But the bubbles of excitement were unmistakeable.

But first she had to face the practicalities. Fraser was out so she called all her children and broke the bad news/ good news.

Chapter 12

Katie nearly didn't answer her phone. Her head thumped. While plying Janey with booze to encourage her to come on the weekend, she'd done the same to herself and was now paying the price. She was debating whether to go back to bed. But she saw Janey's number come up on her mobile so she answered. Janey told her what had transpired.

"So I'll be able to give up work. I could sell the house, buy a camper-van and just take off. But that's a bit extreme, a bit too far out my safety zone. I'll just take my time, invest the money probably and take an income rather than blowing the lot rashly."

"Lucky bitch." Katie was loud in her excitement as Janey explained what had happened.

"God, sorry about your aunt though. I know you wrote to her often and kept in touch far better than I would if I had an aged aunt in Canada. Mind you, if she was going to leave me a fortune…"

"It's not exactly a fortune, but it does mean I can tell Cruella De Ville to stuff her job. Although I'll have to do it nicely, what with Fraser still working there."

"What I wouldn't give to stop work." Katie was envious but delighted for her friend. None of her finest pleading or large drinks or even bribery had worked last night. Maybe now she'd come and join in the fun. "The girly weekend. Will you come with us NOW? I know you've just found out but say you'll come – you've got a whole week left to pack. Please, please, please."

"OK, OK, I'll check today in case I need extra time off, or if I can just leave now, I don't know if I need to work a notice period. But only if I can be one of the drivers. I'm a useless passenger; I'd just fall asleep. I'd be crap company."

"Fine with me, I'll call the others and sort it out."

Katie felt really pleased that at last her friend was getting some good news. God knows she deserved it. Now all she had to do was find them both men. Katie was sure that was the solution to any woman's problems. A decent guy though. Not like the ones they had settled for all those years ago.

Chapter 13

After a whirlwind week and a whole page of instructions for Fraser, Janey was suddenly driving north.

The two cars drove in convoy, Janey and Katie leading in Janey's car, Hilary, Natalie and Angela following in Hilary's. Although there were five of them, they'd decided to take a second car so that they could travel in comfort. And Katie had so much stuff with her.

"Just in case I meet that tall dark highlander," she'd joked with Janey as they'd begun their trip. "Maybe he'll have a brother for you." Janey made a face.

"I don't need anyone to make me happy, thanks very much. Until I decide what to do, I'll be fine on my own."

They'd left on the Friday lunchtime hoping to beat the traffic on the Forth Road Bridge. Once north of Perth, the beauty of the mountains brought a calmness to Janey. She was pleased to be a driver, listening to the happy gossip from her companions. They kept in touch from car to car by mobiles, stopping a couple of times for toilet stops and a coffee. They made good time and looked to be heading for a journey's end in daylight, until a lorry shed its load at Tomatin and held them up for nearly an hour. Although the main route to Inverness, the road was only two lanes wide here so any accident meant a long delay.

"No motorways up here, more's the pity," Katie moaned.

"It's not so bad," soothed Janey, "They won't take that long to clear it, it's just straw. At least it's not a bad accident, or diesel or something. That would have held us up for ages. I've got a flask of coffee and a few sandwiches in the back. Oh, and there's some apples from the garden too. Call the others, there's enough for everyone."

"God, it's like travelling with my mother." It didn't stop Katie from helping herself while calling to the others in the second car.

Janey didn't mind the hold up on the road; the weather was calm and very mild for the time of year. The other drivers got out of their cars and stood around waiting for the blockage to be cleared.

Angela, Natalie and Hilary shared the impromptu picnic, all teasing Janey for being so Mumsie, but none of them were complaining. Even Angela ate half a sandwich claiming the highland air was making her hungry.

"I hope this doesn't happen all weekend," she complained, "I'll be like the side of a house by the time we get back."

"Christ, Angela, if you doubled your weight there'd still be nothing of you." Hilary nearly choked on her sandwich and made the others laugh.

"Very funny, Hil, if you hadn't been late in leaving maybe we'd have missed this hold-up and I wouldn't have eaten anything. I hope they cater for vegetarians where we're going."

"You can always go pick some brambles from the countryside and Janey's got enough apples to feed a small flock of horses with her." Natalie was munching her second sandwich. She had such a busy work and play lifestyle, calories had no meaning to her.

"Stop it you two, yes, they know we've got a fussy veggie with us and a human dustbin, so both of you are sorted. And it's a herd of horses, not a flock," Katie retorted.

"Get you, Mrs Nature, you'll be showing us all up this weekend if you carry on like that." Natalie had them laughing again.

Janey loved all her pals and the easy way they could jibe each other without causing insult.

Snacks eaten, the group got back into their cars and crawled slowly forward in the traffic jam.

Janey had told Katie about some of her plans as they drove. She was glad to get Katie on her own; she knew she could trust her. It wasn't that she didn't want to tell the others, but she didn't want her impending make-over to be the talk of weekend.

"Well now you've started at that fancy gym, there'll be no stopping you. What did you say your posh personal trainer was called?"

"She's called Roxy, and she's not posh. Just because The Club is in Morningside, doesn't mean it's posh. At least I can make use of the big baggy T-shirt my brother sent me after the Sydney Olympics. It hides all the bulges, wine-waist and all."

"You're not that big, Janey."

"Oh yes I am, and don't give me any crap, saying you don't think I've let myself go. I see you looking at me in that way sometimes."

Janey was conscious of Katie watching her as she drove. Janey wondered if Katie realised how much of a crossroads she was at in her life. Good friends often picked up on things like that. Janey knew she'd been quietly different that week. Coming into money that meant she could make changes she'd only dreamt of, gave her confidence a real boost. It had come as no surprise to Katie when she'd shared her plans about the future, even planning a holiday. She'd known that Janey was up to something.

As though she'd read Janey's thoughts, Katie broke the silence, "I've been hoping you'd do something. I thought when you got your wee inheritance you might just give it all to the kids, but it seems to have given you the kick up the backside that you needed to get out of your dull life."

"It's not so dull, just safe. Just too safe. And no, it didn't occur to me to give it all to the kids. I gave them a wee something, but I'd rather invest it, do something with it to help me now and them later. And when I do lose this weight and get back into shape, maybe I'll give you a run for your money in the glamour stakes."

"Well, you'll be richer, but I'll always be younger."

"Only by a month, cheeky bitch."

The chat was good and Janey felt herself relaxing. They drove through Inverness and got onto the Beauly road without any further mishaps. Beauly was a lovely little town. And it had a bookshop, Janey and Katie noticed. They drove through looking for the right road. The turn off to Aigas was well signposted and the road very twisty but glorious. Janey and the girls gave up counting the buzzards they saw; there seemed to be one majestically gliding around each corner. Janey had even treated herself to a small pair of binoculars, hoping to look the part even if she'd forgotten everything she'd ever known about bird-watching.

She listened to Katie's running commentary about all the autumn colours, the houses and small cottages they passed, pointing out lots of thing to Janey who murmured appreciatively even though she could see nothing but the road ahead. And then as she drove round a long, sweeping corner – there it was. Aigas.

Below the road on the next sweeping bend, a glorious Victorian hunting lodge complete with turret, was nestled behind an impressive variety of spectacular trees. The granite stone seemed to glow pink in the sunset. The height of the road gave them a lingering glimpse before the sparkling, granite building bathed in the dying rosy sunlight slipped from view behind tall trees.

The two cars swept up a long, tree-lined drive to be greeted by a huge lawn and circular driveway in the front of the house.

Wow, Janey thought, seriously impressive.

For a mad moment, she had the feeling of coming home. A feeling that grew as they all piled out of the cars to be greeted by the quietly elegant but warm and friendly Lady Lucy, Sir John's wife. As she greeted them, Janey noticed her rose scented perfume. They had something in common already.

"Lady Lucy. So good to see you again." Katie had met Lucy at the Edinburgh Book Festival and, when she'd called to book, Lucy had been delighted.

"We heard about the hold-up at Tomatin, but here you all are now, a warm welcome to our home. I'll show you the dining hall; the food will be ready in about half an hour. Plenty time to freshen up."

Lucy led them into the impressive hunting lodge, far bigger and grander than its humble name implied. A wonderful aroma greeted them and even Angela looked excited at the prospect of food.

"I've given you one of the chalets that sleeps six, so you'll have plenty of room." They followed as Lucy took them back out of the house and led them along a short woodland path and past a few wooden chalets. "There's more chalets behind you and we sometimes have a couple of guests in the big house but I thought this one would be ideal and it's not too far from the house." Lucy stepped up onto the veranda that surrounded the chalet and opened the door. "I'll let you get settled. There's plenty of hot water, tea and coffee in the kitchen and a pint of milk in the fridge. The towels are in the cupboard in the hall where the hot water tank is and there are hot water bottles in the kitchen. This time of year the night temperatures can be a little unpredictable."

"Fantastic, Lady Lucy, perfect, we'll see you at dinner, I hope?" Katie replied for all of them.

Lucy laughed, "Lucy, please, John and I don't use titles here, we're at home. And yes, I'll be joining you for dinner, it's seven for seven-thirty. I don't always because I'm so busy cooking with the others when we have big groups staying, but you're the only guests we have this evening and I love a bit of girly chat. The rangers will be there too so you'll get to meet them and they can help you decide what you'd like to do tomorrow." She turned, still smiling her lovely welcoming smile and went back to the lodge. Once in the chalet, they dumped their belongings, squabbling good-naturedly about which bed each one would have.

Janey didn't care. The warm greeting from their hostess and the chat from her closest friends gave her a sense of happiness that she held very close, just in case it escaped.

"There's loads of books here," Hilary was looking through the bookcase. "We'll not get a peep out of you and Katie all weekend."

Janey went over for a look. "*44 Scotland Street's* here. It's one I've been meaning to read; I've read just about everything else by Alexander McCall Smith. I didn't bring any books with me, but I might just have a wee look at this one."

"Didn't you read it when it was serialised in The Scotsman?" Hilary threw her friend a look of mock surprise.

"Yes, I read one or two of the series, but with not having the time to read the paper every day, I got lost. Never mind, if you lot get too boring, I can go and read."

A fluffy white towel hit her on the shoulder.

"Just shut up and get ready, I'm starving." Natalie was already heading for one of the two bathrooms.

They tidied themselves up and wandered over to the main house. Janey lingered at the back of the group drinking in the beauty that surrounded her. A tall lamp like the kind you see in an old railway station flickered on beside a towering fir tree at the side of the path. She stopped, at once reminded of the lamp in *The Lion, The Witch and The Wardrobe.* This was going to be a truly magical place.

Chapter 14

They entered the house and walked through the large vestibule, which was filled with all manner of curios. Umbrellas, walking sticks, shepherds' crooks and on an old Victorian hat and coat stand with a central mirror, waterproof jackets of all styles and sizes. This led into the most magnificent galleried hall. It was a huge hall. A long dining table and benches ran almost the full length. This was where they were to eat throughout their stay. At the far end of the hall was a sweeping staircase complete with huge stained glass window half way up where the stairs divided to continue upwards to the galleries, which ran either side, high above the diners.

The high walls were covered in pictures, ancient and modern from the Lister-Kaye family and other memorabilia. There were all sorts of stuffed animals and ornaments and a welcoming wood-burning stove. The aroma of food enticed them all in. The gourmet meal, prepared from wonderful local produce, smelled mouth-watering. Their host, Sir John, was there too; a tall, warm, brown-eyed smiling man, pleased and proud to share his home with such a potentially unruly crowd of gibbering females.

"Come on in and get settled. The food's waiting. I hope the chalet's fine for you."

John had a warm friendly voice, one Janey knew she could listen to forever, a voice like melted chocolate, she thought.

Katie answered for them all "Oh it's just perfect, and what an amazing place this is. It's so beautiful, just as you describe it in your book."

"It feels like coming home," Janey ventured, "although my home's nothing like this."

They all laughed.

"Well, we aim to please. Come on, sit yourselves down and we can chat about what you'd like to do tomorrow. There's wild mushroom risotto for you, Angela. All the mushrooms are picked on the estate. Hugh here's an expert."

Five pairs of eyes turned to Hugh. Five pairs of eyes thoroughly enjoyed what they saw.

Wow, thought Janey, this could be very interesting. Hugh came over to them all and introduced himself. He has such a firm handshake, thought Janey. She felt a familiar tingle flow through her and felt bereft when he let go to shake hands with Katie, Angela, Hilary and Natalie.

Here's my tall dark Highlander, Janey thought. I must try to sit next to him. She choked down a giggle at this purely adolescent thought and they all turned to look at her.

"Well Hugh, you still have that special effect on the ladies." John grinned at them all and Janey blushed like a teenager.

"Don't mind Janey, she doesn't get out often." Hilary was laughing, which didn't help Janey feeling even more embarrassed having been so easily rumbled. Hugh sat next to Katie, much to Janey's relief, but her flustering soon vanished and the easy conversation flowed.

They tucked into their meal of goat's cheese and red onion tart, then local roast beef with local vegetables and potatoes and a home-made strawberry cheesecake with clotted cream, washed down with perfect house wine and even Angela had pudding, much to the amusement of the others. No one had seen her eat as much for years, and they said so.

"Well," she defended herself, "if we're going to be doing all this open-air walking and stuff, I don't want to be fainting from hunger do I?"

They were invited in to John and Lucy's vast lounge for their nightcap. Another huge log fire crackled cheerily and the large, comfy couches and chairs beckoned to the well-fed troop. The room was home to a grand piano bedecked with family photographs and boasted two bay windows with magnificent drapes.

Curtains seemed an inadequate word to describe them. Janey felt like she was in heaven. She wasn't as vocal as the rest of the group, preferring to listen to the laughter and gossip and sip her drink, taking in the relaxing mood, which seemed just as heady as the fine malt she cradled. She thoroughly enjoyed "people watching" and often fancied she had a knack for understanding folk just by observing.

"Deep in thought, are we?" Janey hadn't noticed Hugh coming to stand beside her.

"Just really enjoying the evening. It's so relaxing. I can't believe we've only been here a few hours. I feel like I've been here forever."

"Ah, that will be the Aigas magic weaving its spell." Hugh smiled at her and she could feel the warmth in his voice. "Once it gets to you it won't lose its hold. I came here for a few weeks and that was four years ago."

"How did you find this place?" Janey was getting bolder as the splendid malt worked its own magic.

"Oh, I first came here for a summer season while I was at university. Then I travelled and came back. This place is so special, it was in my blood. I'll never tire of the views."

Janey felt so relaxed with this friendly man beside her. He re-filled her drink and they sat beside the crackling fire on a huge faded red couch, which threatened to swallow her up in the deep soft cushions. Janey wished she's been working out and calorie counting for a lot longer before meeting this hunk.

"I was at college too, once." Janey felt herself feeling good, despite her body hang-ups. He was being so nice. She was already looking forward to walking the moors with him the following day. "What part of the highlands are you from, Hugh?"

"Oh, I'm no highlander, but I won't be too insulted, a lot of folk make that mistake. No, I'm from Shetland. Most of us don't even consider ourselves to be Scottish we're so far away from the mainland. I think of Scotland as my adopted home."

Janey wasn't sure if he was really offended, but then he broke into a grin.

"Just teasing, I've adopted the highland lilt, to disguise my Viking ancestry."

Janey smiled too, enjoying the easy chat. "What did you do at university?"

"I was at Aberdeen doing Marine Biology."

Janey nearly choked on her drink. Mixed feelings arose.

"Are you OK, Janey?" Hugh leaned forward with concern.

"It's fine, really. It's just – oh this will sound bad, but I'm divorced."

Hugh looked puzzled. "Not sure I'm with you."

"God, it's not a proposal." Janey laughed at his expression. "No, it's just that my first husband – only husband, he did Marine Biology at Heriot-Watt University in Edinburgh. That's how I met him. I was doing nursing and we got to use the student union because we didn't have our own one. I even lived in Oban for a while after we got married. He worked on a fish farm."

"Small world." Hugh's expression changed fleetingly. "I didn't really do anything like that. Just came here as a graduate, then went abroad and did some diving then came back here for a season and here I am. Do you still live in Oban?"

Janey thought his smile had become a bit forced and that he was making an effort now to look relaxed. "No, we're all from Edinburgh. I – we came back when my oldest son was a baby. My lovely laid back, tolerant marine biologist decided to join the police in Edinburgh and get a brain transplant."

Hugh was looking uncomfortable. Janey couldn't understand what she'd said. She tried to re-capture the easy chat.

"No – I just mean, he changed. For the worse. But I've three lovely kids." Oh god, she thought, I'm making this worse by the second. She tried again. "Have you any kids? Or a wife?" No, the hole was clearly getting bigger, judging by the look on his face.

"So you've contacts in the police?"

This was the last question Janey expected. "Not so much now. It all fell apart a long time ago." Janey was struggling. Even her wine waist seemed to be swelling by the second and she was feeling decidedly uncomfortable.

"Sorry."

Janey wasn't sure if he was apologising about her broken marriage or the sudden awkwardness that had come between them. "No problem. Sorry if I've said something." she ventured.

"No, it's just me. Sorry. Been a long day. I'll go now. Early start in the morning."

"At least you don't have far to go tonight. It must be good living so close to work." She couldn't work out the look Hugh gave her as he said goodnight. Almost of distaste. Maybe he didn't like divorced women. Or women with families. Or fat women. Maybe he'd just been doing his job and being chatty. Then got bored with Janey's prattling. Anyway, she guessed she'd blotted her copy book with her dark highlander.

"Hey, why on your own?" Natalie plonked herself beside Janey. "Thought you'd be chumming hunky Hugh to his cabin the way you two were getting on after the meal. And all snuggled up here getting cosy by the fire."

"Well I'll have to improve my chatting up. Whatever I said certainly scared him off. Anyway, he said he was tired."

Natalie raised one of her perfect eyebrows. "I'll need to sort you out. Can't have you letting eligible men slip away like that you know."

"How do you know he's eligible?"

"A girl can ask. John happened to mention it. At least that's what I thought he meant. Just in passing. Not in direct conversation. I have my means of getting information. Anyway, Mr Hunky doesn't look that tired. I think you may have some competition in the romance stakes."

Janey turned in the direction of Natalie's gaze. Hugh was deep in a laughing conversation with Katie. She was giving him close attention, flicking her hair, accepting another drink and smiling at him. Clearly the two of them were enjoying themselves. Janey felt a rush of jealousy.

"I'm not interested. He's obviously like one of these men on the cruise ships – there to please the ladies as part of his job. I just don't know what I said to annoy him."

"Don't worry, Janey, you've got all weekend to get back in his good books. Anyway, the party's over for the night and Casanova's leaving."

"Goodnight." Hugh waved to the room and Janey was sure he gave Katie an extra wink as he turned to leave. She had no chance against Katie's well-honed charms.

Janey chatted with the girls a while more, the strange conversation with Hugh forgotten for the time being.

"One for the road?" it was Katie's favourite phrase and one they were all willing to comply with to round off the evening.

Measures were generous and they helped themselves to their drinks. They filled in the "honesty" book with what they'd taken as this would be added to the bill at the end of their stay. It all added to the feeling of being at a real home from home. Such a comforting atmosphere and the generosity of their hosts added to the homely and cosy feelings surrounding them all. She decided this was the place for decisions to be made and for the rest of her life to start. She lingered behind the others in the light of the railway lamp on the way back to the cabin. Janey felt like she'd been there forever, far away from the humdrum life she led in Edinburgh.

She saw someone leave the house and jump into a Land Rover. It was Hugh. Where on Earth was he going at this time of night when he lives in the staff chalets, Janey thought. She was beginning to think her dark highlander was just a bit mysterious.

Chapter 15

Hugh crunched the gears as he swept down the driveway and drove home.

He knew his fellow workers thought him strange for not living in the ranger accommodation unless he was on call, preferring to go back to his own isolated home five or so miles away. He resisted the suggestion of party nights in at his solitary bothy, indeed none of his colleagues really knew exactly where he lived. Except his boss, John, and he would never say to anyone. John understood Hugh's reasons for keeping to himself and he respected that.

Life was easier if other folk kept their distance. The less they knew about him the better.

Although he was a loner, he enjoyed the company of Aigas' guests. He liked listening to the constant babble from the groups that visited. He enjoyed teaching the children most, their wonder at the abundant wildlife from the tiniest beetle to the beavers Aigas had introduced with huge success to the estate. Every one of them went home with a sense of having had a great adventure.

Another evening over, he thought. Not a bad one either with that group from Edinburgh. That Katie was very entertaining. Great figure too for her age. Not that I want drawn into anything right now. But a little light dalliance was always a distraction. Not that he would break the rules and get involved with the guests. That was strictly not on. It was a useful rule at times, one he'd hidden behind on several occasions. Katie would be good fun this weekend. He smiled to himself, then frowned, remembering Janey.

She had an ex who'd been a marine biologist, which was a coincidence. And lived in Oban too. An even closer coincidence. And her ex was a policeman. That was way too close for comfort. Hugh didn't want anything about his past to be revealed at the moment. He had too much to lose. He really thought he'd covered all his tracks. He wondered if he was being followed. He hoped not. Everything had gone so well for the past while. Sometimes he even felt relaxed. Janey seemed far too nice to be sent by anyone to find him now. She'd never have said anything if that was the case. God, he was getting paranoid now. That was the disadvantage of the long drive home. Too much time to think. He'd have to be very careful all weekend. At least there were five of them so he could avoid that Janey woman more or less. He hoped he wouldn't have to move on. Not after four years. Not when he was feeling safe and settled. Not now. He'd tried other jobs, fish farming on Loch Creran, near Oban on the west coast of Scotland, but he'd left that after several years and an uncertain marriage. Nowhere else felt like home.

That whole experience had made him more guarded and, some would say, a loner. But that was what Hugh liked. He'd left Oban and travelled abroad, working in diving schools around the Mediterranean putting the scuba diving qualification he'd gained at university to good use. But colourful and exciting as the seas were there, his first love was diving off the Scottish coast, cold as it was. He'd tired of the warmer climes and the visiting women looking for romance and commitment after two weeks.

Oh yes, he had a lot of good memories and one Scottish woman in particular that he'd been very fond of. Although they'd met in Majorca, she'd come back to visit him a few times from Scotland where she lived, then had seemed to vanish and all his attempts to contact her had failed.

She'd loved his dark good looks; "rugged", she'd called him. And when they'd slept together it had been the best for him. If he closed his eyes he could still feel her soft smooth skin against his and the rising passion in her as he gently and softly stroked all her secret places as she'd taught him. She'd been very open about sex and Hugh had found himself, despite his age then, mid-forties, somewhat of an amateur until she showed him a better way to make love. He still wondered what had happened.

They'd parted on a promise that he would come back to Scotland for a long holiday and they could consider if they had a future. He'd have returned home for her but she didn't contact him and when he'd tried to contact her, she'd left her home and changed her phone number. He'd not really settled abroad after that and headed home anyway.

Sometimes, he thought to himself, it's like I'm hoping to just meet her by chance. And it's a better chance if I'm here.

Och, nonsense, he chided himself yet again. That was all in the past. He should be looking to the future instead of yearning for the past. And as he knew only too well it was better to keep some things strictly in the past. He missed the companionship that a good, happy relationship might offer and promised himself he'd make things work out next time.

On his return from his travels he'd come to visit an old friend from University. Betty has been a real bookish type then, studying English. She was from a farm in the south west of Scotland and almost as shy as Hugh. But they'd formed a close if a bit unlikely friendship and they'd kept in touch after graduating and he'd been to visit her on his return. She now ran a bookshop in Beauly, aptly called "Betty's Books".

Despite what he considered a silly name, she'd made a real reputation for herself and her shop all over the country, specialising in local authors and Scottish authors and helping them to publicise their books. He was surprised she was still single, as Betty had come out of her shell since university and enjoyed her job and life enormously.

He'd arranged to meet her in the local Lovat Arms pub, and she'd introduced him to some of the locals. Although, he'd thought, not many of them actually came from the area originally, just like him.

David, some whiz in finance, was an advisor to John at Aigas and when that came up in conversation, Hugh thought he'd see if there were any jobs going so he'd contacted John and had been welcomed back as a ranger for a season. That was four years ago and for the first time in a long time, Hugh felt at home.

Chapter 16

The weather promised to be very kind all weekend. Even though Saturday was their first full day at Aigas, Janey found herself allowing her rusty brain to dig deep and unearth a surprising amount of information about the countryside much to her surprise and Sir John's praise. And much to the hilarity of her friends who were amazed at her tentative knowledge and accused her of swatting up.

The estate was run by a team of rangers who took groups like Janey's around the vast landscape doing all manner of things from fungi hunting, bird watching, bog-walking and cooking. The Rangers were a good crowd and all seemed to get on well.

Janey's favourite, of course, was Hugh.

Although nothing had come from their first cosy conversation, Janey liked him and was pleased for her friend Katie that he clearly fancied her.

Janey knew exactly the kind of experience she'd like to share with him, but her chatting up skills were clearly flawed because try as she might, he was having none of it. She'd have to give in gracefully to Katie as the mutual attraction was obvious.

Still, he'd do as fantasy fodder. Even if she had the feeling that he wasn't all that he seemed.

She could see why Aigas was known around the world as a centre of excellence for naturalists. There was even a loch and areas of natural woodland, the ancient Caledonian Forest, which John was keen to preserve and continue planting with trees native to Scotland.

"Come on you lot." John's voice broke through Janey's musings.

"Don't let a full breakfast make you sluggish, we've eagles to see today. It's a bit misty at the moment, but the sun is on its way, so perfect for the hide. We'll walk past the lochan and I'll chat on the way. Just ask about anything you want. Lucy has your packed lunches ready, and if you need binoculars of walking poles, help yourself by the front door."

They all got their gear together, taking waterproofs just in case the unpredictable autumn Scottish weather caught them out. They chatted as they walked through the wood beside the house and past the huge hen coop, waving to Lucy as she fed the occupants and gathered the eggs. Janey felt better than she had for a while. Even breathing the fresh air, fragrant with pine and fallen leaves, lifted her spirits. John was pointing out all sorts of hidden treasure, as his keen eye spotted things that would normally be missed on a walk.

The morning light on the water of the lochan was dazzling. The occasional ripple on the surface glittering like some fairy dance. It wasn't the best time to see the otters, that was a pre-breakfast excursion, but their slides could be seen on the bank, mud streaks from their dens, known as a holt or couch, amongst the vegetation. They climbed a gentle hill up to the bird hide. There were wide ladder steps up into it and it was partly screened by the leafy surroundings. It was surprisingly big and easily accommodated the party of six.

"With any luck we'll see the eagles today, the conditions are perfect for them hunting." Join pointed to the rocky cliff several yards away to the right of the hide. "That's where they nest. This pair has been here for many years and this year they fledged two chicks."

Janey willed the birds to come into sight. After about ten minutes or so, the most magnificent of all the Scottish raptors glided into view. It was breath-taking to be so high up, almost level with the bird. With the binoculars, Janey felt as though she could just reach out and touch it. Its feathers gleamed in the light. It soared on the thermals, hardly beating a wing and in then in the distance came its mate. The birds circled for a while then moved soundlessly up the glen to continue their search for prey. Overawed by the sight, they all left the hide and continued their ramble. After a while, John explained that they were now walking through a Bronze Age settlement. Janey would never have guessed that the narrow, winding paths through grass and heather mounds hid a whole settlement underneath. They stopped to take in the beauty of the glen with its winding river flowing far below them. It was a panorama of the finest Scottish scenery.

"Lunch time ladies, and then we'll walk back through the forest and should be back for afternoon tea. Free time after that and then a trip to the badger hide this evening after dinner."

"I didn't think I'd even be hungry after that huge breakfast, but I'm starving" Janey sat and unpacked her lunch.

"Even I'm hungry and intend to eat everything this weekend." Angela made them all howl with laughter.

"I never thought I'd see the day when I'd hear you say that Angela. Why, you might even put some weight on." Katie nudged her friend as she sat on the blanket John had provided for them to sit on.

"I think I'm doing plenty exercise to avoid that," Angela retorted.

The walk back to the house was an easy amble through the ancient forest with John pointing out the different trees and talking about them. The autumn colours of the deciduous trees were beautiful as the afternoon sun filtered through and there was a hush in the forest broken by the occasional rustle in the undergrowth and the sound of snapping twigs as they strolled back to the lodge.

After munching fresh scones with butter and jam, Janey took herself off back to the cabin. The stove had been lit, even though it wasn't particularly cold outside, and Janey was soon snoozing in the armchair.

She awoke to her giggling friends coming in, ready to go to dinner. They all walked over to the big house, and as they opened the door, the aroma of a hearty meal greeted them. John, Lucy and the other staff members were already there.

Hugh managed to manoeuvre himself beside Katie. They chatted happily through most of the meal and Katie was clearly smitten. Janey felt a pang of jealousy.

I'm being ridiculous, she thought. Katie is my friend and Hugh obviously prefers her company. She pushed the little green-eyed-monster to the back of her mind and concentrated on the conversation around her. John was explaining the history of the centre, from its' beginnings as a fifteenth century house, to its' transformation as a Victorian hunting lodge to the magnificent building it was now. Parts of the roof had been missing, after it has fallen into disuse; it had taken a lot of time, effort and love to re-build it. Janey was fascinated and couldn't wait to see more of the house and the surrounding estate. The meal over, they relaxed for a while over coffee and then John announced that it was time for the next event.

Hugh escorted them all to the Aigas minibus, ready for the drive deep into the forest where they all hoped to see the badgers. They weren't disappointed and there was a bonus for them when the pine martins appeared, relishing the peanut butter smeared on twigs and giving quite a show. The hardest thing to do was for them all to keep quiet.

The experience of being so close to these wild animals had the desired effect and they'd all shut up.

Leaving happened far too quickly for Janey. They woke early on the Sunday and all went to hear John give a talk about Aigas over breakfast. Janey promised herself she'd come back as soon as the spring season opened. And she meant it. Not just the draw of the strong silent highlander – he was clearly Katie's now, she was only human after all – but being at Aigas had awakened something in her that she liked. She couldn't wait to return. Hugh had been right. This place had magic.

Chapter 17

Janey listened as she drove homewards as Katie waxed lyrical about Hugh and her determination to go back to see him.

"He's a really nice bloke, don't you think?" Katie was sounding Janey out as they drove home.

"Katie, he's lovely and clearly interested in you. And despite what you all might think, I'm not interested in him – he's all yours."

Janey thought about the conversation. She was really keen on Hugh after the Friday meal, but he had hardly spoken to her since. No more or less than the others and they'd all enjoyed a good laugh while on their nature ramblings. Katie told her she'd had decided to take the initiative and given Hugh her number and suggested she could come back. Not as a guest at Aigas next time though. Katie told Janey that she had worried this might have been a bit presumptuous at the time but Hugh's reaction had apparently brought out one of his sunniest smiles.

Katie told her what Hugh's reply had been.

"I've a friend in Beauly; she runs a bookshop, "Betty's Books". There's a wee B&B above her shop that is very good. I'll call her and let you have the details."

Katie grinned at the memory.

"I think I remember driving past that one." "You know Janey, I'm sure that under other circumstances he'd have kissed me goodbye. I wished he had. And a whole lot more. But the waiting will make it all the sweeter if – no, when – it happens."

"It's a long drive for uncertain sex." Janey laughed at her friend as the chatted.

"There's no uncertain about it." Katie protested. "If he calls I'm going back to see him. And there's always the train. They're regular to Inverness and there's a station In Beauly.

No problem. And I can check out the bookshop too. Hugh told me Betty comes to the Edinburgh Book Festival every year. So, I have something in common with one of his friends already."

"Well, at least if it doesn't work out, you won't have to worry about bumping into him in Edinburgh."

"Oh ye of little faith." Katie was indignant. "I have a very good feeling about this."

Katie snuggled into the passenger seat and Janey heard her breathing get regular as she drifted off to sleep. Great company, Janey thought. A loved up dreamy forty-something. Janey hoped for her friend's sake she'd find some highland happiness.

Chapter 18

A week and a big bank transfer later, Janey had made her mind up.

She could afford to pack in her job – so the letter went to the manager who'd made her life so difficult recently – one of these high flyers who thought they knew everybody's job better than others and made Janey feel really inadequate even though she'd been working in the supermarket for years. She'd miss the people she worked with but would see them as she shopped so that wasn't too hard. That had been a scary decision, but she felt so much better for it. And she'd booked that holiday to Majorca as well.

"What do you think, Katie?" Janey felt she should phone Katie and share her news.

"I think it's a brilliant idea. The weather will be quite warm still and let's face it, Janey, when did you last go abroad?"

"I went to Portugal once, but that was a long time ago. Iona had her eleventh birthday there. I remember her being so embarrassed when the waiter kissed her on the cheek when he brought her birthday cake to the table."

"Well then, you go for it girl. Do you want me to come with you?"

Janey hesitated and Katie began to laugh.

"Too much hesitation I think. It's fine, I think you'll enjoy the experience alone. Anyway, I'm toiling for leave from work till the end of the year. Trying to save days for a couple of long weekends for the Highlander."

"How's that going?" Janey was relieved her friend understood about her going away on her own.

"Fine. We speak on the phone a lot and I'm going to see him next weekend. Staying at the B&B above Betty's shop. It's great; she does this book swap thing so I won't even have to take books with me."

"Like you're going to do much reading." sniggered Janey, "Unless it's bedtime reading of course."

"Ha, ha, very funny. But I must say that's the plan. I've even treated myself to some new undies from the new Bellissimo shop beside Harvey Nicks."

"Don't forget your thermals as well. If he's into the outdoor life you might need them."

"Just because I'm trussed up in walking gear doesn't mean I should wear big pants underneath."

Janey was pleased for her friend. A bit of romance was just what Katie needed.

"I'm almost jealous of you going back there. I've actually been thinking of applying to Aigas to be a volunteer."

"Well Janey, it could be just what you need. A complete change of scenery. John was really impressed with your interest and you made the rest of us look really thick with some of the things you knew. They were saying when we were there how difficult it is to get folk to work the winter season."

"Oh, I'm not sure about being a ranger, I thought more about helping in the kitchen or around the house."

"Get the letter written, see what they say. The worst that could happen is that they say, 'No Thank You'. And I can come and see you when I'm there. I won't be able to keep Hugh in bed all the time – I'll have to let him go to work sometimes."

"Well, if I do manage to go, Fraser can look after the house while I'm gone; I can hardly commute. A four-hour drive to work is a bit excessive. I'm sure I'd get inexpensive accommodation out of the summer season. And it would be good to have a friend visiting, although I suspect when I tell Fraser, he'll be up to visit too, what with his obsession with Scottish history."

"You go for it girl, nothing ventured and all that."

Janey was glad she'd shared her thoughts with Katie. Her up-beat attitude really helped.

She rang off after some more girly chit-chat and sat down to write to John. She didn't have a CV or anything and it was a long time since she'd applied for a job, but she also included that she'd been going to the gym regularly and was feeling the benefit already. And so she was. Roxy was a slave-driver, but in the best possible way. Janey was already beginning to see the shadow of a waist and she'd gone down a couple of dress sizes. Roxy was into Pilates and callisthenics as well as "visualising" her muscles. Janey visualised so much, she should be stick thin by now. But the encouragement Roxy gave her and the comments from her family and friends were giving Janey the sort of boost she wished she'd had years ago.

The awful sadness that had plagued her a few weeks ago was lifting. She had a holiday to look forward to, just a few days, get a bit of colour and hopefully she could work at Aigas until Christmas. She'd have to come home then; all the family were staying for the holiday.

Janey sat at her computer and googled Majorca. What a good googly feeling that was.

Chapter 19

Fraser had been a bit shocked when she told him she was packing up her job and going on holiday to Majorca. She'd never really travelled on her own. In fact, she'd NEVER travelled alone. He'd been a bit wary of this. His ma, alone in a foreign country.

"What if something happens to you?"

"Don't be ridiculous, Fraser, plenty of folk travel alone. You went to Australia last summer and travelled alone apart from staying with Uncle Tony. Nine weeks you were away and you came back safely. This is just a few days. And you'll enjoy having the house to yourself. Just don't trash it. No parties."

"No problem," Fraser grinned. He never let her down. Well almost never. There had been that time he'd sworn blind there had been no party when she'd been away for the weekend and put all the ornaments back in the wrong places. A bit of a give-away that one. Still, at least he'd thought of putting them away to keep them safe. She'd caught him fair and square that time. "Anyway, the best parties here are the ones with you and all your mad girly mates. We can have a party when you get back. Show off the tan and stuff."

"Excellent idea. It's a deal. You look after the house and I'll have a party for your mates too, when I'm back."

Fraser thought how lucky he was to have such a good mum. Not when she was nagging him about his room or moaning about washing clothes he'd found on his floor, which were in fact perfectly clean but fatally crumpled in a heap. She was OK. And it was true – she threw a mean party. He was so glad of the change in his mum. She looked happier, less care-worn than she had for ages. And trimmer too. He'd only hinted at that. Wasn't sure how sensitive that might be with her.

Women could be touchy about that sort of thing. He'd spoken to his sis about it. She'd said to be tactful, whatever the hell that was supposed to mean.

Anyway, he could crank up the music, get his mates round for a few beers, have a bit of a jam with the guitars and only have to wash up once. Nice one.

Chapter 20

Well, Janey thought, "Here's to me." It was a major step for Janey – a holiday on her own. Child and man free. She felt so brave and adventurous. What utter luxury. She sat in the sun at the Gran Café in Puerto Pollensa in Majorca, sipping gin – export, of course – and fresh orange. The breeze made it so comfortable as she languished there waiting for the bus to the old town of Pollensa. She was hoping the Sunday market was on. She ordered another gin – feeling quite mellow.

Already, her plans were taking place. She'd come here – alone – as a kind of test. To see if she was OK being by herself. Everyone thought she was mad, of course. Embarking on an adventure at her age when her life seemed so settled. For "settled" Janey saw "boring".

Janey thought her life was definitely getting boring. Safe, but boring. And anyway, she thought she was ready for change. She'd been in Majorca for less than 24 hours and already she'd managed to avoid being captured by well-meaning couples. The kind that latch on to you and try to include you in all their activities. Janey could do without that, she intended to enjoy her own company and do exactly as she pleased.

The bus came. Janey climbed on board. It was almost full. Mainly holiday makers (all couples of course) but quite a few locals. That was what was such fun with the local busses. A great chance to "people watch", and much cheaper than the taxis.

The scenery was lovely – the bushes of bougainvillea tumbling at the sides of the road, all beautiful vibrant colours; the quaint Majorcan buildings; small farm dwellings with their orchards and rows of tomatoes, olive trees and other vegetables growing in the warm reddish soil; and every so often, huge, luxurious villas, some with pools.

The old town of Pollensa wasn't far on the bus. A small town steeped in history with narrow streets and some lovely quaint shops. And of course, all the cafés perfect for the hot traveller. With all their bright umbrellas and cheery waiters beckoning to her to try their delicious coffee and Majorcan pastries. She decided to go to the market first.

The market started in the main square then ambled up the narrow twisting streets that led from it. The choice of fruit and veg was amazing. Janey almost wished she was staying in self-catering instead of half-board so that she could cook some of the exotic fish she saw. But the hotel was her treat to herself. No cooking for a few days would be another first.

Janey got to the bottom of the El Calvario steps. They climbed straight up, looking steep from where she was right - at the bottom – of all three hundred and sixty five of them. Of course, she was climbing them at the wrong time of day - midday - her and all the other mad tourists. Maybe the two generous gins were a bit of a mistake.

Trying to make it look as if she was choosing to climb deliberately slowly up the steps, Janey did eventually make it to the top. She really would have to shift some more weight. She'd have to make sure she didn't slip into the comfort zone for these few days. She'd managed to get clothes for her holiday sorted out without buying much. She hoped the exercise and healthy eating would help her to continue to lose a bit more. She felt worse than she had for ages.

Her weekend with the girls had been fine. Baggy walking trousers and big jumpers hid a hell of a lot. But now her womanly bulges were definitely turning into womanly curves. Much better. Womanly bulges did not look cool in shorts.

Although, Janey didn't care too much what she looked like at the moment, because no one knew her here – she'd had these shorts for years and no one would notice the undone top button concealed by her baggy t-shirt. If she was to seriously contemplate going back to Aigas to work, she'd have to get fit. Maybe not back to the size eight she'd been in her teens, but a bit more weight would have to go.

That was the problem with being abroad; baggy jumpers were out of the question.

At the top of the steps she took in the panoramic view, savouring the breeze. It was amazing. There was a little chapel, which was deliciously cool inside after the heat of the midday sun and the climb. It was easy to understand the tradition of climbing the steps during Lent, symbolic of Christ's climbing the hill on Calvary, carrying the cross. Although not particularly religious herself, Janey enjoyed learning about the local customs and appreciated the symbolism of climbing the steps. At the tiny café beside the chapel, she resisted the tempting rosé wine and had a refreshing cup of tea – black from now on with lemon and no sugar – then she ventured down. Janey stopped half way and saw a wonderful textile exhibition. She'd love to do some of the crafts she saw there and at the market. She'd studied art at school and sewing, knitting and craft were sometimes hobbies she enjoyed when she had the time. Janey was always looking out for ideas.

Janey finally made it down the steps, where a mobile made of clay leaves and driftwood – in the most wonderful shade of green, caught her attention at one of the stalls. She sat in the shade of an umbrella, ordered a fresh orange juice and checked out the photos she'd taken. She was loving her new camera – so easy to use. She'd treated herself at the airport.

She'd even read the manual. It would be strange going home with no photos of herself. Probably just as well for now. Janey found it odd not talking to anyone else, but the sense of freedom was incredible. Two of her buddies, Katie and Natalie had sent good luck texts – what a fortunate person Janey was to have such a network of good friends.

Chapter 21

Janey really did find it very strange being on holiday by herself. Back at the apartment in the hotel she sat for a while on her balcony. Even the birds in Majorca seemed different. There was Mr Blackbird who behaved like a tree creeper climbing up the trunk before hopping onto a branch and doing the more normal blackbird thing of wobbling his tail. The sparrows were reassuringly the same. Hopping close to her balcony– hoping for a stray crumb. But they hopped closer to her than at home with the continental charm of the flirty waiters – and generally got the extra crumb.

Janey was enjoying just watching the different people. From the safety of her balcony she saw "The Cyclists". The place was a haven for them, almost always in groups of four or more. Lycra clad padded shorts, firm abs, cycle sculptured glutes. Janey was like that at twenty. Before the kids, when she was first married and living in Oban, she could cycle the twisting glens on her twenty-one-speed silver Peugeot racing bike, no bother. Her muscles had been so trim the doctors couldn't turn her first breech pregnancy. Then there was the day she passed for half fare on a Morningside bus, when visiting her parents back in Edinburgh, at five months pregnant. She'd been shopping with her mum – how they laughed when the bus conductor just gave her mum the tickets. No questions asked. Then she spotted the "Fit Couple". They didn't need the golf style buggy to transport their luggage to their villa room – no – they did it themselves, power walking behind airport trolleys. He was stick thin – she was all big ass, slim waist and bouncy tits – chatting as they tried to out walk each other.

Mind you, Janey thought, my ass is wobbly big.

Janey wanted to do something to keep fit on holiday, maybe swimming every day and a bit of walking. The hotel had groups that went on organized walks. She would join in.

The pool beckoned.

She knew glass wasn't allowed close to the edge of the pool so she'd got her empty plastic bottle of Fanta Limon – washed out of course – and poured a minibar rosé into it. Which meant she could sup surreptitiously without breaking the glass rule. The real diet and exercise would continue tomorrow. The last time Janey had drunk alcohol out of a plastic bottle she'd been sixteen. The memory made her smile.

Another crowd of friends in another time zone.

If only her parents had known what their good little girl from her posh all-girls school – James Gillespie's High School for Girls of course – did on a Saturday night when she was meant to be round at Hilary's house watching TV.

They'd meet in Morningside, that poshest of areas in Edinburgh where folk thought SEX was for keeping your coal in, and Sandra would go into the off-license for cider. Janey would have a small bottle filled with little bits of various different spirits nicked from her parent's booze cupboard. They hardly ever drank so she'd reckoned on them not noticing; but the mixture tasted disgusting. Everything was there – vodka, gin, whisky, brandy, crème de menthe etc. And they think teenage binge drinking is a new thing nowadays, Janey thought. Nonsense – Janey and her pals had invented it years ago.

The cider drowned the taste of the vicious cocktail then the five of them would nip into the Plaza Ballroom before the bouncers realized they were drunk. The Plaza had a no booze policy and everyone was searched before they could go in. Looking back at the memory, Janey couldn't remember if they were good times or not – just all part of growing up.

And here she was doing another bit of growing up; she wondered if folk ever really stopped growing up.

As Janey sat by the pool, she thought about her future.

The holiday alone seemed to be working and by the time she got home she'd find out if Aigas would accept her for some work.

She knew her family would be surprised when she shared her plans, but she was looking to her future and being a bit selfish for a change. She thought of Scotland on a warm sunny day, in the beautiful highlands, surrounded by some of the world's most stunning scenery in that remote and wild place. Even with the rain and wind, just being in that glorious part of Scotland was magical. From the high mountains to the vast, remote, white beaches, the country had a depth hard to describe. The sea might be freezing but its colours touched the soul. Each day in that part of the world brought different colours and changes – and she knew she could be happy there. She'd miss her coal fire and her family. But being at Aigas they could visit.

She had thought she might rent out her house. It would give her an income but now that she had her inheritance she'd be able to leave Fraser to look after the house. If and when he moved out, she'd worry about it then.

And, she resolved, if she walked to the shops at home, instead of taking the car; that would help shift the bulges. It was only a ten-minute walk after all; she had just got lazy. Janey was really looking forward to swapping her dull, boring, very samey life for something much more fun.

Chapter 22

The book she was reading as she sunned herself was called *How to Kill Your Husband*.

She'd picked it up at the airport and as folk strolled past her at the pool she'd drawn more than one comment. Not that she had a husband to kill, and she felt only deep pity for her ex now, with all the things he had passed up on sharing with their kids. But the book was very funny.

In all these kind of books, there was always romance of some kind.

Janey wasn't sure if she needed romance in her life. Janey was quite happy with her singledom. When she thought about it, she was quite lucky really without a significant other to think about. Maybe she was becoming quite selfish in her middle years.

There had been one or two pleasant enough men she'd dated. But none of them lasted. It seemed to her that the first flush of romance was great, then as routine set in the men got more and more boring, less romantic and full of fun as if they just didn't see the need to keep trying any more. Instead of charming her with how much they were looking forward to seeing again, little facts that were glossed over at the start began to creep in, like "I meet the lads every Friday – you don't mind do you?" or "I play golf most Sundays – and Wednesday evenings – you'll be OK meeting up with the girls then won't you?"

God Almighty, Janey thought – that's far too close to marriage. She thought about Hugh; she was glad Katie was getting on so well with him. She still wondered what she'd said to put him off, but here in the sun it didn't seem important.

Back at the apartment Janey had a wonderful luxurious bath before a stroll before dinner – how classy she felt.

Packing for one was so easy. She got to take only the stuff she needed. No packing and trying to remember stuff for someone else in case they forgot. Another reason to be single. That would make a good book, *100 Reasons To Be Single*. But she was no writer. Janey thought there were lots of advantages of holidaying alone too.

How she would enjoy evenings of TV of her own choice. She could spend the dying hours of the night listening for the cicadas and not the snores or farts of a fellow traveller.

No, she thought, she'd usually holidayed with compromise as her watchword. This time, on her own, she was able to go to dinner and not only get to choose exactly what she wanted to eat in the hotel restaurant, she didn't have to share or be influenced by a travelling companion.

Maybe she could come back to Majorca, assume a new identity, do clay and jewellery making, be a market trader, live in a camper van. But no, she'd go back home and live her dream.

She set off for dinner, a short stroll in the warm evening to the main block of the hotel. The place was full of visitors in varying shades of sun-tan. From the pale faced to the clearly overdone – ouch she thought.

Then it was back to her room for great British TV all evening and a wee nightcap of Majorcan gin – lovely.

Chapter 23

Janey found it was a strange few days – calm and unhurried. She couldn't remember when she'd ever been away and not had to worry about anyone else. What a luxury. She could watch from a distance the hassled parents with toddler in tow and just give them a "glad it's not me" smile.

She'd always holidayed with the kids around Scotland. Caravans on farms, log cabins, beach bungalows and lots of "piles of rubble". Janey couldn't understand the attraction of taking kids abroad when they were young. Always watching out for them: worrying about sunscreen; rests in the heat; getting enough water down them; eating late, and of course, the tantrums. Far harder work than being at home. All that was behind her now.

Janey was approaching fifty. The menopause, which she suspected was not far away, was beginning to kick in. It was an odd time of life for women, the end of fertility. After years of worrying about periods, contraception, moods, no moods, children, no children, this part came with mixed feelings. For Janey, she looked forward to the freedom of not having to worry about contraception – on the rare occasions that sex was an opportunity. But Janey knew of friends who for whatever reason hadn't had the inclination or opportunity to have children and who felt they might have somehow missed out now that nature would have her inevitable way.

Janey was glad she'd had her children. Even though she'd started when she was very young compared to a lot of women nowadays. They'd made her into a better person. She'd been frustrated at times with them all from time to time, but they'd taught her patience and given her a good perspective on life.

How she'd worried about them when they were little. When they'd been ill or hurt, she felt it too. When they'd celebrated – she was the happiest mum in the world. Janey was very lucky to have her grown-up children as her friends.

Her three kids were all fine, all of them pretty much standing alone. Almost. Not a big enough "pretty much" to keep Janey in Edinburgh.

So, all things considered Janey was doing just fine.

Janey went to Puerto Pollensa on market day on the Monday, which was lovely and different from the old town market from the day before and only a few minutes away by bus. She enjoyed all the markets. She walked slowly, browsing the varied and colourful stalls around the square. A light shower of rain began. It was perfect for walking through.

The brief outburst sent the stallholders scurrying with military precision to protect their produce.

Janey paused to watch as plastic sheets were swiftly placed to cover the open stalls. One stallholder even took another's table under their packed canvas until the shower passed.

Umbrellas appeared like magic, tourists, including herself, were welcomed under covered stalls – clearly nothing to do with the purchases they might decide on while being sheltered by accommodating stall owners.

The shower passed, goods were uncovered, plastic and umbrellas all whisked away and as the sun shone down once again, peaceful chaos was restored. That was how Janey felt. The holiday was lovely and peaceful, but she knew it would be chaos once she returned home.

The market place buzzed with many languages. Even a whole range of British accents.

"Been shopping?" A large lady with a dark wrinkly tan greeted friends. Three or four friends greeted each other at Café L'algar where Janey sat enjoying the pastries, coffee and rosé wine.

"How could you come to Puerto Pollensa and not shop?" was the reply.

Janey disagreed. She was having more fun sitting there watching and listening to the chat.

She wondered about the couples she saw. Some chatting amicably, some pouring over the guide books or maps, planning the rest of their stay. And then there were the ones sitting in silence. No chat, hardly even looking at each other. Were they bored or just being quiet, lost in their own individual thoughts. Well, I'd rather be on my own than bored with a partner she thought.

Would she like to turn the clock back, rub out all the marriage troubles and start again?

Janey had a wee word with herself before any gloomy thoughts disturbed her comfortable seat in the sun. Despite the heartbreak, nothing could make up for her gorgeous children who she loved and respected with all her heart.

She was moving on, changing her life and whatever obstacles were thrown in her path, she'd deal with them and look to the future. And the future would be on her terms this time.

Chapter 24

Everything happens for a reason – and sitting here, alone, was turning out to be great therapy for Janey. Being away from home with no one to talk to meant she only had her own thoughts to listen to. She had space and time away from the dull routine to sort out in her own mind exactly what to do. She couldn't remember ever having so much time to think. It was certainly an eye-opener and she could highly recommend it to anyone. She dragged herself up from the sunny spot she'd found and strolled down to the sea front. To her left was the beautiful shady pine walk and to her right, the bustling marina. She decided to take a stroll amongst the boats. There were all sorts. Little dinghies used by the owners to get from their yachts to the shore. Small Majorcan fishing craft with their distinctive square sail that could be turned to make an excellent shade over the boat from the sun. The Sunseekers owned by the mega-rich and the usual diving and glass bottomed boats. Janey wasn't really concentrating as she wandered in the warm sun.

Then one of the posters advertising SCUBA diving made her stop. She knew the face on the poster. It was Hugh. She was certain of it. The poster was a bit faded, but she'd know that face anywhere. She remembered he'd said something about working abroad. He must have been here. Her heart skipped a beat. He'd worked in the same place as she was now.

A blonde, tanned 'Adonis' approached her.

"You like to dive with me?"

Janey ignored the obvious double-entendre and smiled sweetly. "Not for me thanks, but I think I recognize a friend who used to work here." Only a slight exaggeration, Janey thought, her curiosity aroused. "What's this diver's name?" she gestured at the poster.

"Oh, an old photo Señora, He not here now." His accent was heavy, but Janey understood.

"Yes, I know." said Janey patiently. "But what is his name, he looks so like my friend."

"That's Hugh The Jock, he gone long time ago, you dive with me now?"

"No, honestly." Janey said. "It's just if that's him, he's back in Scotland now, I saw him a few weeks ago."

"Ah, back to his little wife in Scotland. Back to his fishing village. We knew he missed her." The Adonis continued to leer hopefully. "We men need our Señoritas."

Janey was gobsmacked. She stared at this Adonis. She felt a shiver despite the hot sun. "Of course." She managed to squeak out. "Good to have met you." She turned before he could engage her again.

Married. Married. Of course! That would be why he drove off each evening at Aigas. But John had suggested to Natalie that Hugh was available. It didn't make sense: Natalie must have misunderstood. Maybe John meant Hugh was available for walks and stuff. Trust Natalie to pick up the wrong end of the stick. *Married.*

Then what in Gods' name was he doing inviting Katie up to Beauly for the weekend. And another thing, was that why he'd changed his attitude towards her so quickly when Janey had mentioned Oban. "Fishing village" her Adonis had said. To a foreigner, Oban might sound like a fishing village - it was where the finest seafood in Scotland was landed. Had Hugh lived in Oban?

Hugh must have moved from there to the Highlands to be at Aigas. Maybe his wife was a secret? Maybe he was a serial philanderer and kept his wife safe in some remote bothy? Janey's imagination was running riot. She calmed herself. There must be a sensible explanation. But there was obviously more to the dark highlander than either she or Katie thought. It would certainly explain his sudden coldness towards Janey when she mentioned Oban. Janey felt goose bumps on her arms rise despite the heat. What was going on?

What on Earth would she tell Katie? Friendships have been lost to the bearer of bad news. She'd have to know. If it was Janey getting all loved-up and hopeful and Katie found out Janey's prospective bed partner was married, Janey would want to know.

She desperately wanted to call her friend, but hated the thought of telling her over the phone. Janey was only away for a few days, she'd tell her face-to-face when she got back. Katie would be back from her first weekend with Hugh by then.

Maybe he'd come clean. Maybe he was divorced and hadn't wanted to say anything to Katie over the phone, after all it seemed to have been a long time since he'd been in Majorca and a lot can happen in four years. You see, Janey chided herself, lots of perfectly plausible explanations. But why freeze her out at the mention of Oban if he had nothing to hide?

Chapter 25

Janey was back on a local bus heading back to her paradise in Majorca. She was trying hard to shake off the uneasy feeling she had after discovering Hugh was married. She'd concentrate on her fellow passengers instead and try to forget what she'd heard. Plenty time to contemplate what to do when she got back from her trip. It was quite a journey back in the local bus. It had been really busy and Janey had had to stand all the way back. Standing next to her and holding on to the top rail was "Model Man". She'd never seen a man in the flesh with shaved armpits. She'd seen plenty in "adult movies" but then they usually have shaved trousers parts as well. Being a total stranger and clearly foreign she didn't dare ask him. Of course, Janey thought, that would be foreign compared to her. He would probably be local where she was clearly a tourist. He had strange thin shaved lines on his almost girly face. Girly with the firm jawline, slicked but tousled dark hair and eyelashes that Janey would kill for. She tried not to stare. But those shaved armpits really let him down. He was clearly displaying a severe case of shaving rash. Why show it off – not a good look – don't men check before they leave the house.

She was musing on this as she left the bus. She was feeling very hot and sweaty and clearly not the picture of model-like prettiness. She'd dashed in, had a pee then glanced in the mirror while washing her hands, turned sideways to check if her wine waist had magically vanished because she'd been walking around the town that morning and horror of horrors. Her upper back was sporting the tattoo of "lonely and holidaying alone" in white tiger stripes across her back.

She wondered whether she had been looking like that every day. She wanted to dig a large hole and sink slowly into it.

She thought she had the perfect solution to getting the sun tan lotion on the bits of her upper back that can only be reached by someone else, given that she was not double jointed. She liked the "once a day" sun-tan lotion. It stuck to your skin, but applying it single-handed was no easy task. Too much and you get the white tattoo look. Not enough and you burn. The lotion goes on – you dry for ten minutes – fifteen to be safe and then you're OK for the rest of the day. It had always worked for her – but there had always someone else to a) put it on and b) check for streaks. Janey reckoned if she'd put it on face cloth and sort of flicked it onto the unreachable area, it would soak into the cloth. So instead, using all her girl guide intuition, she decided if she squirted it in an evenish line across the top of her back and used a non-absorbent item – in her case a shower cap stretched between her upper right shoulder and lower left arm, she could spread the lotion evenly, allow to dry and all would be well. This had worked reasonably well, or so she had thought. No wonder she'd been getting such sympathetic stares. And Janey thought it was because she clearly looked single and interesting.

At the pool, and now streak-less, Janey put her stuff on a sun-lounger. Tummy in – as far as possible – shoulders back – check labels are all under control. It was such a good feeling, she thought, a real feeling of freedom.

Janey swam breast stroke and tried to do it perfectly. She used to swim competitively at school and with all the practice she was getting, she felt confident in the water. She did four lengths of the lagoon pool. The pool was very large compared to other hotel pools she'd seen. Janey guessed it must have been a hundred yards long. Or maybe a hundred metres. Janey tried hard to convert to metric. She tried to do the metric thing when baking or shopping. Working in the supermarket gave her good practice. But when it came to distance, she was just plain old-fashioned.

Janey realised way too late she still had her contact lenses in. But there was no going back. She got to the side of the pool in a perfect set of strokes and carefully opened one eye – no – far too full of water. She couldn't rub it – the lens would fall straight out. She tried blinking – but her other eye wouldn't even open so she turned her head casually towards the sun – like it was all meant. Janey was hoping the sun might dry out the water in her eyes even though they were tight shut. She blinked carefully – and her right eye opened. It worked; the lens was still there and her eye was still working. But her left eye was still swimming. Janey closed it and turned her head sunwards for a bit longer. Eventually her left eye seemed fine and the lenses were still there. Janey should have known better and should stop showing off while wearing contact lenses. That demon drink. Janey climbed out of the pool, showered and lay on the sun lounger basking in the Majorcan sun. She wondered if she was the only Brit who showered after swimming. It was clear that it would take a great deal more swimming to shift the flab.

She dried herself off and headed for the bar, a slave to the rosé wine. The lovely Manuel served her the chilled house rosé. She tried to be super smart and have the correct money – nine euros. He was aghast – it was only four euros twenty for a half litre. Manuel explained that Janey was getting confused with the price of full bottles of rosé wine at dinner.

And then the perfect family landed on her left.

An English family – not that Janey was biased. Her mother had been English and she'd always supported them as long as Scotland weren't playing in football/rugby/golf. Janey felt it was ridiculous that the Scots should be so hostile to their down south neighbours. Then – the Perfect Father spoke, replying to the Perfect Child. Janey guessed she'd be about ten. Ten and clearly spoilt.

"What's for lunch?" the girl asked.

"Oh god, you're not going to moan are you. All you do is moan," Perfect Father retorts.

Perfect Child was sulkily silent. She clearly wanted the last word. "Not if they've got chips."

She sat, and leaned her chin on her hand refusing him eye contact. Janey was pleased she wasn't the only one who had occasional, dysfunctional conversations with her children. Perfect Child then started cooing over the hopping sparrows that were enjoying the outside dining bonanza. Janey overheard the dad telling her they were chaffinches. She suppressed a snigger by quaffing her chilled rosé. Maybe I'll do all right at Aigas after all, she thought. Perfect Family was served their lunch. Janey overheard the mother telling the lovely Manuel, "That spag bol wasn't what I expected" – *what is there to expect?* Janey thought - spaghetti and sauce. Perfect Mother wasn't best pleased. Perfect Child didn't like the lettuce in her tuna sandwich, but ate it reluctantly once Perfect Mother had removed every shred.

"Why is the bread toasted?" Perfect Child demanded.

Janey felt like tapping her on the shoulder and explaining that in the Rt. Honourable Lord Sandwich's Rules didn't extend as far as Majorca. But Perfect Father beat her to it.

"They don't know how to make sandwiches here, so we have to eat like the locals".

True Majorcan cuisine, the toasted tuna sandwich, thought Janey. She would have preferred roast suckling pig. Perfect Child transformed in Janey's mind to a sweet, fat piggy. All juicy chops and a twitching snout. Reality snapped her back as she watched Perfect Child greedily wash her lunch down with gulps of coke and greasy handfuls of chips. In fact, the Perfect Family ate a plate of chips with, of course, traditional Majorcan tomato ketchup. Perfect Child had a wine waist to match Janey's even though she'd only be about ten – or was it a pot belly? And then – Perfect Child rounded off her traditional lunch with ice cream. That at least was a local speciality. Janey was half way through her half litre of wine – time for a dip and a snooze.

Over by the pool, Janey spotted another woman who looked almost the same size as her slipping into a bikini and using a towel as a completely inadequate modesty wrap. No, Janey reckoned, she was bigger, round the waist. And her shoulders were burnt whereas Janey's were tanned nicely and Modesty Woman had cellulite. Really, Janey chastised herself. This wasn't solidarity for womankind; she could be a real bitch sometimes.

Chapter 26

The rest of the day passed without event and after a lazy evening, Janey slept deeply. She was woken with an almighty crash at four in the morning. Startled for a few seconds as she adjusted to the sudden wakening and unfamiliar surroundings, Janey sat up in her bed. It had only been thunder.

Janey got quickly out of bed, chilled in the air-conditioned room. She pulled her sarong around her and opened the balcony door. The hot, humid night air hit her as she ventured out. A magnificent forked flash greeted her followed swiftly by the crackle of thunder. She could feel it through her feet. Janey loved thunder and lightning, she always had. Even as a child she found the power and magic of it irresistible. She curled herself on one of the armchairs on the balcony to watch the free display provided by the mysterious power of Mother Nature. She found herself remembering her childhood and how her dad told her to count slowly between the lightening and the thunder to work out how many miles away the lightening was. She'd done the same with her own children.

Somehow it made the thunder less frightening and more of a game. Even to a child, one mile seems a long way away.

Janey revelled in the loud noise and spectacular forked and sheet lightening, feeling almost disappointed when it faded and the steady rain began. She lingered a while, enjoyed the sudden change in energy with the onset of the cleansing rain. She could smell the heavy rain on the warm dry ground and on the grass. It was sweet and fresh and she knew when she got home, closed her eyes, and remembered the smell, it would transport her back to this magical place and time.

The balcony was under cover so she was able to sit, protected but feeling part of the powerful weather.

She went back to bed, lulled into a deep sleep by the drumming of the rain.

When she woke, the sky was clear, and so was she. She was going home to whatever life decided to throw at her. She was looking forward to the start of the rest of her life.

Chapter 27

Palma airport was busy. Janey felt very lost there on her own. It seemed like everyone knew where they were going except her. For a few moments she felt like this was a scene depicting her life. All these people with a purpose and she was confused trying to read the directions. Queues everywhere and she was struggling to find the correct one for her. Maybe this travelling alone was just too much for her. She could feel the panic rise up. She even thought for one awful moment she was going to cry. Janey hadn't felt like that for a very long time.

She'd had such a good time away, full of fun and planning – all very exciting – and here she was now, one small person surrounded by people who didn't even know she existed.

Janey sat down on one of the airport seats. She took a few deep breaths and had a serious word with herself. This kind of self-indulgent wallowing simply would not do. She was made of sterner stuff and considering the life changes she was about to make, it was hardly surprising that she would have the odd wobble. Just not in the middle of Palma airport with a plane to catch.

The threatening lump in her throat eased, along with the wobbly legs and rapid breathing. She was an ex-Girl Guide for god's sake.

Janey stood up and took a deep calming breath. All she had to do was check in her luggage, find a wee corner to settle down until her flight and fly home. Part of her wondered if she'd ever get used to travelling alone. But a much bigger part of her was pleased she'd got this far. She knew with a bit of guts and determination she could carry out her plans. There would be far bigger obstacles to overcome, she thought, than a busy airport. She still had to decide what to do about the information she'd learned about Hugh. And how to broach it with Katie. She'd worry about that later. When she was safely home.

Feeling calmer, she found her queue, checked her bag in and headed for security. She always felt intimidated by the airport security. That she somehow had to act innocently, even though she wasn't guilty in the first place. She thought it was probably because she had to empty her pockets, take off her belt and shoes and put her hand luggage through the machine. A bit like entering a prison. Not that Janey had been in prison, but like most folk she'd been a couch observer of many crime programmes. She got really nervous going through the scanning thing. Either her silver bracelets or her watch always seemed to set the alarm off, increasing her guilty feeling. This time she'd taken them off and put them with the other things in the tray.

Two steps to freedom, she thought, suppressing the urge to giggle as the stern Spanish security people – complete with guns – stared at her. Giggling would draw their attention and she already felt unusual as a lone traveller. No bleep. Free.

Belongings retrieved and the threat of being clapped in irons now past, she headed for the airport departure lounge and a welcome gin and tonic. Or two. Janey was determined to enjoy her flight home. After all, who knew what would await her on her return.

Chapter 28

Only two messages on her answerphone. A huge pile of junk mail. All the usual utility statements and a party invite. But there was a letter from Aigas.

Before the kettle had even boiled, before a bag was opened to unpack or the phone messages listened to, Janey sat on the bottom of the stairs and stared at the envelope. This could make or break her future. Well, the future she really wanted.

Janey supposed that there were other choices she could make. That was the story of her life though. Really wanting to do something but having to put it on a back burner or perhaps never do what she wanted because she had to compromise and think of others. She really hadn't had time to do much for herself. She seemed to have spent all of her adult years looking after and thinking about others. And once the kids were old enough and able to do much more of their own thing, her parents had been unwell. First her dad, then after he died, her mum, who only wanted to follow her husband as quickly as possible. In the quiet house, sitting on the stairs, still with that surreal "home from holiday" feeling, Janey could almost hear her mum. She certainly had a strong sense of her presence. She could feel her mum urging her to open the letter and not worry about what it said. Just to go with the flow because if it's meant to happen, it will.

Her mum had a saying for it. "What's for you won't go past you."

Janey opened the letter. It was hand written by John Lister-Kaye himself.

"Dear Janey,

What a pleasure it was to have you and your friends stay with us recently. We are all very glad you had such a good time. You brought a lot of laughter to Aigas.

I had the feeling you were pleased that you remembered so much about the beauties of nature that we're so lucky to have here.

And thank you for buying a tree. These have been very popular with a lot of our visitors and I approve of your choice of the Gean tree – the native cherry – you must visit it often and see it grow. I have a feeling we helped plant a few seeds for you too.

You were lucky to see the badgers on the same night the pine martin decided to visit the hide. You are quite right when you say that the most difficult thing is to keep quiet while they're out to see us – even now, I find it hard not to shout out with excitement, and I've been seeing that sight for years.

Your letter interested me, as we usually get work requests from students studying in this line of work."

Janey's heart sank, that was something she hadn't thought about – of course they'd only take people training in stuff to do with nature. She reluctantly read on.

"However, I was so impressed with your enthusiasm and the way you got on with all our family and staff here at Aigas, that I'd like to offer you the chance to join us in the house. I know it's not as glamorous as being a ranger, but your knowledge of cooking and your clear ability to get on with people would be an asset to our team. You'd also be free to join in with the rangers as they take out the groups. I'm sure you'd quickly pick up a lot of knowledge and could even be a ranger assistant if you wished."

Janey grinned from ear-to-ear – it was a yes. She hardly cared what she would do – she'd scrub floors, chop wood and do the mending if that was what was needed – IT WAS A YES.

"However, before we could take you on, you'd need to do a first aid certificate. We all need to have them. If you call me, I'll let you know which training centre is nearest to you.

We look forward to hearing from you,

Warmest wishes,

John"

Janey was ecstatic. This was when she missed the dog in the house – he'd have jumped up with her, wagged his tail for Scotland, run around and around to catch it and probably have barked his head off. Then he'd have begged for treats, he'd have loved Janey jumping up and down.

Janey was going to do it – she was taking the first steps forward with her plans.

She looked at herself in the mirror; already looking so much better.

She'd get on the phone to Roxy as soon as she could. Janey had a real challenge now and she knew Roxy would share her good news and keep helping her get fit.

She'd have a cup of tea, unpack, call the children and then get going on the phone. And then, best of all, they'd have her resignation letter at the supermarket by now. Her bullying boss would soon have to find another dumpy housewife to annoy.

Janey was going to Aigas.

Chapter 29

Janey called John at Aigas the next day. They talked for a good hour or so and even though she suspected all the things John had said were meant to put her off and test her to see if she really meant to come and work, they just heightened her resolve. She'd need to get a medical just to check that she was fit to work at the centre. Her doctor, Moira, would be pleased she'd taken her advice and had lost weight. She could hear the doctor's words the last time she went.

"Your weight just doesn't match your height, Janey."

She'd known her doctor a long time. She had children of a similar age to Janey's.

"I know, but the temptations in the supermarket are just too much. And sitting alone at night doesn't help the nibbling. Maybe I should take up smoking."

"That would hardly be sensible," her doctor had laughed. "I can get you an appointment at the weight clinic if you need extra help."

"No thanks, Moira, too many fat folks there. I promise I'll try this time. I know exactly what to do, you know, I was a nurse once upon a time."

"Not all nurses are skinny. It's not a given you know what you need. A little knowledge and all that…"

"Fine, fine, I hear what you're saying." Janey had promised the doctor she'd try.

Moira would be pleased.

She'd need a tetanus jab as well. Hers was probably well out of date. Janey was fairly sure it was nearly ten years since her last tetanus. She'd had to keep up with them with working at the supermarket, but she knew it had been a while. And a flu jab was advisable. John had suggested a place where she could do her first aid certificate.

It was in Forth Street in the town centre. Across the road from Radio Forth, the local radio station. Now that was an exciting place, Janey thought. Janey could still remember her excitement at meeting Leonard Cohen as she waited outside when he was visiting the radio station prior to playing at Edinburgh Castle. She was at the front of the crowd in the street and had even managed to shake his hand. Janey had seen him play at The Usher Hall when she was sixteen, and loved his music and poetry ever since. What a lovely, husky voice he had. What a shame it was that she'd never meet him again... Katie had been at Radio Forth, but then Katie had done all sorts of things Janey would never have had the courage to do. Still, maybe Janey was finding some of her old forgotten courage and some of the adventurous spirit she'd had as a sporty teenager. She wondered what the girls would think of her plans. She hadn't told anyone except Katie; they all thought she had a screw loose going to Majorca for a few days on her own – what would they think of her going up north to work at Aigas. The thought of Aigas and Hugh reminded her she'd need to speak to Katie soon.

Janey hoped that being a co-worker wouldn't be a problem for Hugh. She hoped that working with him would thaw his polite but distant manner and she could show him how much fun she could be.

Especially if there was a perfectly rational explanation for what she'd found out and particularly now that he and Katie were an item. She'd hate to lose Katie's friendship just because Hugh didn't like her.

The sooner she spoke to Katie the better.

So once she'd broken the news to her family, she'd let the girls know. Then she'd deal with the fall-out. The uninvited advice and, she hoped, the eventual support of those nearest and dearest. They'd finally realise she was quite capable of de-rutting herself.

Janey still found it strange to think that, barring disasters, she'd never have to worry about money again. And if she dwelt on it too deeply she felt quite guilty. She knew that her aunt would thoroughly approve of her actions and that Janey wouldn't squander her windfall. Janey felt she had her aunt's approval in some strange way. Maybe Aunt Bridie and Janey's mum would be on some cloud or other willing her on. Janey knew that with the celestial support of those two she had the finest pair of guardian angels a girl could want.

Janey called the first aid place next and booked her course. They'd had a cancellation so she could go the following week. Now that she'd started the ball rolling, she just wanted to get everything done so that she could get a starting date sorted out. After years of feeling her life was the same old boring routine, Janey was looking forward to her self-made challenges more and more each day.

She'd already called Roxy who was delighted with Janey's news and she was seeing Janey that afternoon to sort out another programme for her to follow at the gym. All her ex-husband's comments about her weight had hit home over the years and Janey knew she felt quite vulnerable about it. It was time to stop feeling that way about herself. Firming up the womanly curves was a must. And she was well on the way.

Chapter 30

"Janey that's brilliant." Katie was sitting at home, sipping a chilled glass of wine when her friend called. "Bloody brilliant, you'll love being up there. I had a fabulous weekend with Hugh. The underwear was a roaring success, and the sex fantastic. I'm a born again virgin."

Janey just didn't know what to say. Katie sounded so happy that Janey didn't want to burst her bubble.

"And I'm going back in two weeks. Hugh's so busy just now he can't get the time off for a weekend down here."

I bet he can't, thought Janey, a bit stuck for words.

"Hey are you OK? I thought you'd be pleased for me. What's with the silent treatment?"

"Nothing, nothing, just tired after all the travelling." Janey's courage deserted her. She just couldn't bring herself to say anything to Katie, not over the phone. *I'll wait till I'm with her and then tell her.* "Hey, let's meet up at the weekend and catch up. I'll bring the wine and get a taxi over to yours."

"Great, I'll see if any of the others fancy it. Make it a girls' night in."

Janey's heart sank. She'd never be able to say anything with the other girls there.

"Fine, see you Saturday then, usual time." Janey feigned enthusiasm.

"Definitely. And I'll do some nibbles. Need something to soak up all that wine. You can show off your tan, all I've got is wind burn and grass stains on my bum."

Janey just didn't want to hear it. She gave a suitable laugh, said goodbye and put the phone down.

What on earth was she going to do? She would be at Aigas herself in a couple of weeks; maybe things would be clearer then. She could try speaking to Hugh herself, get him to tell

Katie he was married or had been married or whatever the hell was going on. She'd thought about it long and hard and it seemed she needed to find out the explanation. It was just unfortunate that Janey had seen the old picture in Majorca and found out about Hugh from the swarthy Spaniard.

And for very selfish reasons she thought that if she told Katie now about her suspicions, and she relayed it back to Hugh, it could jeopardise Janey's work at Aigas, and she certainly didn't want that. It might be easier if she waited until she got there and maybe the situation would be clearer. Janey certainly hoped so. She and Katie had been on the receiving end of errant husbands before and it wasn't a good feeling. Janey didn't want to be the one to take the sparkle out of Katie's eyes. She'd put it all to the back of her mind, enjoy the girls' night, it would be the last with her pals for a while, and she'd try not to get drunk. Oh how the demon drink can loosen tongues, she thought.

Chapter 31

"Just go, I'll be fine." Fraser was trying to get his mum out of the house to the waiting taxi. "At this rate you'll miss the train. And there won't be another one for ages."

She was still trying to add things to the more than comprehensive list of Do's and Don'ts she'd already issued him with.

Fraser had been surprised that his mum had decided on such an adventure at her age. The trip to Majorca had been out of character, but this was something else. Traipsing off on a whim to cook and clean in a big house in the middle of the highlands just seemed plain daft to him. But there had been a big change in his mum recently. Not just the health club stuff – which he had to admit, was working – but she was much more confident. He supposed he'd got so used to her quiet ways, not really voicing an opinion about anything, that this new mum was quite strange. Not in a bad way really. If he thought about it, he'd probably taken her for granted, expected her to be there, looking out for him. No, if he was honest, this was much better and certainly took the pressure off him when he eventually moved out. She'd had a long chat with him. Explained how she was feeling and although the money had a lot to do with her sorting things out and making big life changes, it hadn't changed her. But Fraser saw a change. It made him feel a bit insecure if he was honest. Not that he'd say anything to his mum. She needed him to tell her he'd be OK. Anyway there was Don and Heather in the Borders and Iona in Stirling. They weren't all that far away. He felt a bit choked while watching her pack and being so excited. Maybe he was just being selfish.

He'd always thought his mum would be in Edinburgh if he needed her. These are crazy thoughts, he sighed, and only half listened to the instructions she was giving him. He hoped she'd written them all down. She would have of course. God, she'd even told him about where to get her will if anything happened and where all the insurance policies were. That really freaked him out. He really had to face facts; he just didn't want her to go. Talk about a generation exchange. He'd played out this scene before in his imagination, only it was him moving into a flat and his mum being all gushy. Now it was him telling her to look out for herself and keep in touch.

He shook himself as he helped her into the taxi. She looked like an old hippy backpacker with her rucksacks and a holdall. He smiled at the thought.

"And what's so funny?"

"Nothing Mum, but don't you think you're too old for this hippy, nomad stuff?"

"Thanks for that, but no, I'm just spreading my long unused "hippy" wings a bit. Being adventurous. I will miss you though, very much. It feels a bit odd me leaving and you waving me off."

"Ditto, but we'll cope. Anyway, first chance I can I'll be up there. It's a great excuse to go back to Inverness. Even if I do have to sleep in an earthen floor in your bothy."

"I think you'll find it's more of a luxury log cabin, central heating, real beds and running water."

His mum smiled that smile she saved for him. He could feel the lump in his throat. He hugged her hard, kissed her on the cheek, breathed in that special smell just as he had when he was little and she was cuddling him.

"Go and enjoy, just don't mess with any mad highlanders. Call me when you get there."

"I will. Love you."

"Love you too Ma." He used the term of endearment without thinking as she closed the taxi door and as always waved until she was out of sight. It doesn't really matter how old you are or how long or short a time someone you love is going away, there's still that sting to your heart. Fraser stood for a while, then turned back to the house, took a deep breath as he walked into to his neat and tidy home. How the hell was he going to keep it like she'd left it? Well, she'd trusted him to look after things and he wouldn't let her down. Christmas wasn't that far away, and he'd said he'd visit. And it was good to see her so happy. He had to remember that. She'd always encouraged him, so now it was his turn to return the favour. He saw now that she needed more in her life to... how had she put it... fill the empty nest. He'd just have to make sure she'd have a tidy nest to come home to.

Chapter 32

Janey's heart broke as the taxi drove away. She wondered for the umpteenth time if she was doing the right thing. She knew she was, but it had been a lot tougher than she thought leaving Fraser. She knew it was just a mother thing, but his face as she was getting into the taxi made her heart ache. Her wee laddie. She took a breath and held it, willing the tears to stop. This was ridiculous, she chided herself. You're nearly fifty, he's an adult and a very capable one; he's a lovely lad, he'll be fine. She forced a smile, wiped her tears and let out the breath. You're going to be alright, she told herself. And Fraser is too. And he's only a phone call away. She wondered if it would have been easier if all her kids had been there to see her off as they'd wanted too.

"Mum, I can take a morning off and come through." Iona had been adamant.

"Nonsense." Janey had been just as stubborn. "I don't need an audience when all I'm doing is going north for a while. You can come and see me whenever you want. Stirling to Inverness doesn't take that long even on the train, so stay at work. In any case Fraser will be there to make sure I really go."

She'd had a similar response from Donald and Heather, and had fobbed them off as well. Maybe she'd been too hasty, maybe Fraser would have liked to have had his brother and sister there. I'm just being daft, she thought. They will all be fine. And I will be too. The taxi was approaching the city centre. Edinburgh was full of road works, especially in the centre. All folk did was moan about the disruption the building of the trams was causing. Janey fancied the idea of the trams. She'd liked them in Dublin when she and the girls had gone for another of their weekends. And Iona had sung their praises when she'd worked in Amsterdam for a while when she'd been travelling. The folk in Edinburgh would love them when they were finished. But there was no doubt the roadworks were causing a real headache in the city centre.

The taxi drove along Princes Street, the main city centre road. It was full of folk getting to work and already very busy. The shops were getting ready to open. The gardens on the other side looked lovely in their autumnal colours, and for all the years she'd lived in Edinburgh the sight of the castle, high up on its hill overlooking the gardens never failed to impress her. We have a truly beautiful city, she thought, feeling nervous but not so emotional. It was a wrench leaving, but it wouldn't be for long, just until Christmas when Aigas closed until the spring and she'd been touched by the good luck card the girls had signed for her last weekend when they were at Katie's. She smiled at the thought that Fraser was planning to come and see her. He loved the whole area around Inverness; they'd visited there often when the children were small. It would be good to see him. The cab passed the Scott monument. It was a long time since she'd climbed the three hundred and sixty five steps to the very top, the same number as the El Calvario steps in Majorca. She'd be able to do it much better now. She remembered the looks on her children's faces when they'd got to the top and how pleased they'd been when they got their certificates to say they'd been all the way up the steps. Iona had been terrified; she'd never liked heights, and had refused to look at the magnificent view, clinging to her mum instead. Iona had never got over her phobia of heights. Janey smiled at the thought, Iona had missed out on a few good views over the years, but at least she'd had a go.

Stopping at the taxi rank inside Waverley station, Janey paid the driver and looked for the platform. She heaved the big rucksack on her back and carried the smaller one and her holdall. Maybe Fraser had a point, she did look like a bit of a middle-aged nomad, but matching luggage would hardly have been practical to take to Aigas. She'd tried to take only the essentials and at least she wouldn't have to bother with hairdryers or straighteners or much make up. Katie would have found it impossible to pack for a trip like this; she'd have had to have packed the whole car. Janey felt cheered at the thought of Katie. She'd be coming up to Aigas in a week or two; it would be good to have her there.

Janey found her train, coming from London Kings Cross travelling north to Edinburgh then on to Inverness.

She'd pre-booked her seat and was pleased it was at a table. True to form she'd brought a packed lunch and nibbles for the journey. Even a flask of coffee, the flask would be put to good use where she was going. The warmth of the train was soothing, she'd probably have a snooze on the way unless her book was so gripping she wouldn't be able to put it down. She suspected it would be good, Ian Rankin's latest thriller. It had been hard not to pack loads of books, but she knew there was a considerable library at Aigas. She hadn't been able to start *44 Scotland Street* on the girly weekend, they'd just been too busy. And there was always that bookshop in Beauly, she looked forward to a browse and coffee on her time off.

Janey had thought about taking her car, but she would be able to drive the vehicles that belonged to Aigas so there didn't seem much point. Fraser had promised to look after her wee car, he was a good driver. The car would be there if he needed it. He didn't use it often, but she was sure he'd be careful.

The train was passing the other big station at Haymarket and making its way towards where Janey lived. Shame it didn't stop at her local station, which would have been much handier. But this train swung onto the north line and was soon chasing through the countryside.

She settled with her book, the train was surprisingly quiet, so no one had joined her. She was quite glad, she just wanted to be with her own thoughts, not listening to the ramblings of a stranger. For once she wasn't in people watching mode, just looking forward to her own private challenge and happy with her own thoughts.

Her only troubled thoughts, apart from leaving home, were about Katie.

The evening at her house had been full of fun and laughter with Katie taking centre stage with her new romance. The girls had quizzed her as only women can do, suggestions getting more and more outrageous as the wine flowed.

Janey had felt a bit uncomfortable when she arrived at Katie's that last Saturday. It had been just the two of them for the first half hour and it had been on the tip of Janey's tongue to tell Katie what she'd found out about Hugh in Majorca. But, as Katie had chattered on, Janey hadn't the heart to say anything and spoil the evening. Then the moment passed as the others arrived. Janey decided she'd wait until she'd be at Aigas. Maybe she'd find another explanation but she doubted it. Surely if Hugh had been married before and divorced he'd have said something to Katie by now. From what Katie had said they'd talked until the cows came home. Maybe it should have been "until the deer came home" she thought randomly.

"He was a lovely lad. Katie had cooed to them as they sat round her cosy lounge munching on nibbles and sipping wine. Janey had been strict with herself; she limited the amount she drank in case the booze loosened her tongue. "And he was such a gentleman."

"You mean he said 'please' before he asked for sex?" Hilary brought a roar of laughter to the room.

"No, I mean he held open the door of the car, restaurant, whatever, paid for our meal out, refused to let me pay for anything."

"So you paid him in kind instead." This time Natalie joined in.

"No, we talked a lot, in fact he was so good to be with I found myself really opening up to him. We really seemed to connect."

"That's a euphemism for good sex if ever I heard one." Natalie challenged, almost choking on her wine.

"It's really none of your business whether we had sex or not." Katie tried very hard to be indignant but her friends knew her too well.

"So the huge grin and rosy glow is all due to that pure highland air?" Janey was caught up in the banter and found herself relaxing.

"Not so pure if you ask me. But then our Katie's not all that pure either," Hilary had caused another outburst of laughter.

"Hey, you lot. Call yourselves my mates, disparaging my pristine character like that. It's been so long since I had any decent sex, I'm a born again virgin."

"Ah, so not any more, tell us the gritty details, is he a right highland stallion then? If those broad shoulders and rippling biceps, not to mention the six pack are anything to go by, I bet he makes for a demanding bedtime companion." Hilary's comments were getting outrageous, but Janey found them very funny.

"Not that I'm going to enlighten any of you, but we didn't spend the night together. He went back to Aigas both nights; he does on call and stuff."

Janey had found herself pausing at this point, but carried on with the fun, she'd been surprised at Hugh not staying over with Katie after she'd made the effort to go all the way up to Beauly. She would have thought he'd have organised her trip for his weekend off. Something just didn't sound right.

The girls had continued to quiz Katie, but she wouldn't tell them any more.

"God, you lot sound the same now as when we were all teenagers, and if you think peer pressure is going to make me give you any more details, you can think again. I'm older and wiser now. All I'm prepared to say is that I like him very much and the feeling is obviously mutual. But it's early days. And now Janey can go up there and really sound him out for me." Katie smiled warmly at her friend.

"Ours will be strictly a working relationship. Anyway I'll hardly see him, I'll be working in the house, not being a ranger." Janey hoped she'd got away with her light-hearted comment and that her suspicions wouldn't come across. Katie could read her like a book.

"Well anyway, we can all go out together when I come to visit, maybe Hugh has a secret brother or handsome pal, we could make up a foursome."

"Back to sex again." Natalie chuckled as she helped them all to a top up of wine.

Janey had been glad the spotlight was off her with the laughter that ensued. They'd continued the evening, outrageously putting the world to rights. Then the girls had produced champagne and the lovely card, which had taken her by surprise. Janey had insisting on opening the bubbles and sharing it with her friends.

"I'm hardly likely to take it to Aigas with me and it would be a shame to keep it until Christmas."

They'd drank her health and continued blethering until their taxis came.

Janey sat with her eyes closed as the train's rhythm soothed her and remembered the happy evening. She'd been glad of the support when she'd shared her plans with her friends. They'd been really encouraging, though god knows what they'd said behind her back. Their friendship meant a lot. She hoped her suspicions about Hugh would be resolved. She didn't fancy falling out with Katie. Sharing her thoughts with Katie unless she was absolutely sure would spell certain disaster for their friendship.

Janey shook herself out of her reverie and looked out of the window. She was nearing the mountains now, all clad in their late autumn colours. The larch golden as their pine needles fell, the evergreen firs, the heather losing its vibrant purple hues and turning the moors into a patchwork of muted colours. The view was wonderful. Janey was looking forward to seeing the dramatic landscape change into its winter coating of snow. Janey picked up her book reluctantly; she could watch the scenery forever. But she'd soon be starting her next adventure. Feeling slimmer and fitter, still with a healthy glow on her skin from the Majorcan sun, she looked forward, sitting as she did on the train. She'd put her worries about Katie and Hugh to one side and enjoy the rest of her journey. Yes, she thought, I am looking forward to the future. I just hope the future's ready for me.

Chapter 33

Katie sat in her office staring out of the window. She felt like a lovesick teenager. Every time she thought of Hugh even her toes tingled. This is quite ridiculous, she thought, especially at my age. I can't even concentrate on my work. I haven't felt like this for a very long time. She felt quite jealous of Janey, who would at this moment be heading north to see him. She checked her watch thinking, she'll be over half way there by now; I wish it was me. Katie took a sip of her coffee, which had now gone cold. God, I can't even concentrate on drinking a cup of coffee, as she winced at the cold taste.

It's not the same as coffee from a flask. The memory stirred as she sat and stared. The picnic she and Hugh had shared when she'd been up to see him. Sitting together on the tartan rug, sheltered from the breeze in a little heather clad hollow beside a gurgling highland stream. She'd snuggled up beside him as they sipped the steaming coffee. The tin mug keeping her hands cosy. The autumn sun had felt warm as they sat in their remote shelter. Hugh had made the formidable task of walking through the bouncy heather seem so easy. She thought he must have known every step of the way as he helped her over the boggy bits and over large rocks on the path. She'd even teased him about bringing all his women here. He'd laughed and told her again there'd been no one but her in all the time he's been working at Aigas. Katie didn't really care if it wasn't true. She was happy to be with him; it was wonderful. Hugh seemed to have the knack of making her talk all about herself. She'd never really shared her thoughts with a man before. Even her ex. They'd married too young and had grown apart, especially when the children had come along. She pushed those thoughts aside and brought Hugh to mind again.

She'd even felt quite shy when they'd made love for the first time. She'd joked to the girls about it and they'd all laughed but Katie really had blushed as she cuddled down in the bed waiting for Hugh to finish in the bathroom. He'd almost seemed nervous too. They'd giggled like a pair of teenagers, which had put both of them at their ease.

She remembered the feelings he'd aroused in her when he'd taken her into his strong, tanned arms and held her close.

"Let's not rush this," he'd crooned. "I'd like to enjoy this for as long as possible."

"You make it sound like this will be the only time," she'd replied as she ran her hands across his chest. His hairs were dark and springy and as she stroked him she could feel his nipples harden. "I'm hoping this will just be the start."

"Silly girl, I know it won't be the last time, I just don't want to rush it this time. I want to remember this as very special for both of us. The way I feel just now…well, I don't want it to be over quickly."

"Shh, kiss me before I faint with passion, you're having quite an effect on me. And we've got all night."

"Katie, I'll have to leave very early in the morning, tomorrow's a working day for me remember." Hugh smiled and drew her close. He'd been fine about using a condom, and had come prepared.

His mouth felt soft but urgent on her lips. His hands on her breasts and his caressing of her hardening nipples brought delicious waves of yearning as he slipped her flimsy nightdress from her shoulders. He bent down and circled her nipples with his tongue before sucking them softly and then more urgently. Katy could hardly suppress the arching of her back as he kissed her all the way down her tummy. He gently parted her legs and explored her aroused clitoris with his tongue bringing her to her unavoidable climax. She was washed with waves of pleasure and passion. He moved back up her body, kissing her now tingling skin until she thought she'd explode again. As he kissed her breasts and then her mouth urgently now, she could feel his hardness as he held her close, and as she felt the waves of lust fuelling her arousal, she knew she was giving herself to him much more than she'd ever done to anyone else. He reached down and felt her soft wetness, and gently entered her. Katy immediately came again. Hugh held himself there as long as he could and when he reached his climax, Katy cried out. Satiated, they lay hot and delighted, wrapped in each other's arms. Their loving had been tender and passionate. Katie had never felt so secure as she slept in his arms.

The only sad time for her was when she'd woken at two in the morning to find him gone. She'd felt a real sense of loss. She hoped it wouldn't be too long before they could spend a whole night together. The memory was still so strong, and as she daydreamed, Katie was desperate to see him again. "Penny for them?" her business partner butted in to her reverie.

"Oh, nothing, just thinking." Katie blushed at her memory and was brought smartly back to reality and the working day.

"All that sighing didn't look like nothing." Tom grinned.

"Could it be that Ice Queen Katie is in love?"

"Get lost, Tom."

"Ah, the guilty blush. So when are you going back up north again? I'll have to watch you; maybe you'll pack up here and run away to the wilderness with your highlander to run barefoot in the heather."

"You are such a townie, Tom. The highlands are quite civilised. Anyway, we could open another branch in Inverness." She grinned at him. She knew what a shrewd businessman he was. And how careful he was with money.

"Steady on, Katie. Let's not get ahead of ourselves. How's the Walkers' stationery coming on? Or have you drooled over the designs?"

"Ha, ha, very funny. It's coming on fine, should be ready for printing by the end of the week." "It'll be the end of next week if you don't start doing some work." The chat was good natured, Katie thought herself lucky to have Tom to work with. "I'm going out for a sandwich, anything you want, or has love stolen your appetite too?"

"No thanks, I've brought in some soup."

"That'll be love soup then." Tom called over his shoulder as he left the office. The pencil Katie threw hit the door behind him and she heard him chuckling to himself as he went down the stairs. *I really have to get on with some work and stop lusting.* She recovered her pencil and tried to concentrate.

"Ten days and I'll be back to see you," she whispered to herself. She'd be pleased to see Janey too. Katie desperately hoped Janey would enjoy her time at Aigas.

"You don't have a problem with me seeing Hugh, do you?" Katie had spoken to Janey on the phone after the girls had come round a couple of weeks before. "You did spot him first."

"Of course not, he's lovely. And perfect for you. Anyway, I don't need romance; I'm off on my big adventure."

"I'm glad you're happy, Janey, you seem to be glowing these days."

Katie smiled at the memory. Her friend did seem so much happier than she had only a few weeks ago. And she was looking much trimmer. Hugh had introduced Katie to his friends at the local pub when she'd gone to see him. They'd all been very friendly. She especially liked Betty, who owned the bookshop. She'd learned that Betty had known Hugh since their university days. Hugh hadn't told her he'd even been to university. But then she knew so little about him. He was great at getting Katie to talk, but she was learning fast that he was hugely private and that she'd have to wait until he felt ready to trust her as much as she trusted him. Betty had said as much.

"I've known him a long time, we were best mates at uni and even I don't know all that much about him. These Shetlanders, all dark Vikings you know." Betty had joked as she nodded towards Hugh bringing their drinks. "Viking man of mystery, aren't you?"

"Not really," Hugh set the drinks down. "Just no time for idle chatter." He smiled at Katie. "Far better things to do than talk."

"Couldn't agree more." Katie had blushed as she smiled back.

"Steady on you two, get a room." Hugh's friend David joined them. "You've certainly charmed our Hugh, Katie. We've never known him bring a lass to the pub have we, Betty? We'd began to think he was much more into sheep."

"For goodness sake, David, don't scare the lass." Betty turned to Katie. "Ignore the lads, you enjoy yourself. It's good to see Hugh smiling and relaxed."

They'd had a great evening and Katie was looking forward to heading north often.

Stop, she said to herself. You're at work and Tom's right. If you don't keep working there'll be no long weekends, just lots of overtime.

Katie took a deep breath and looked at the work in front of her.

The lustful thoughts would have to wait. And anyway, she had a phone call from Hugh to look forward to later.

She'd have to settle for telephone sex.

Chapter 34

Janey changed trains at Inverness. The sun was shining, matching her mood and there was still some warmth in the air. The station was busy, but she had no trouble finding the platform for the local train to Beauly. Although only a few hours from Edinburgh, she felt like she was in another world. She was really excited and looking forward to her new job, but at the same time she felt quite alone. All the weeks of planning and talking were one thing but the reality of such a change was definitely daunting. The Beauly train was half full, clearly used well by the local people. Everyone seemed friendly and she settled down to watch the view. The scenery was stunning. And it was lovely to be able to take it all in, instead of glancing when she last drove to Aigas. The rich autumn colours, the sun glinting on the streams and waterfalls and the high mountains all around gave Janey the sense she was going on holiday rather than to a new job. She was looking forward to meeting John again, he'd called to say he'd meet her at the station and drive her the remaining eleven or so miles to Aigas.

She got off the train and waited on the platform. The station was in the middle of the town. Beauly was looking very pretty in the sunshine. The hanging baskets still looked fresh and the red stonework gleamed. She looked forward to seeing more of the town. Across the road she could see the bookshop she'd heard Katie talking about. And above the shop was the bed and breakfast Katie stayed in when she visited Hugh. Janey was looking around her when she felt a hand on her shoulder.

Hugh. Janey was lost for words.

"Welcome. John sends his apologies, he'd rather have picked you up himself, but he got held up with the estate manager and asked me to come."

"Oh, yes, fine, no problem." Janey knew she was stuttering.

"Yes of course, good to see you again." Now she knew Hugh must think her mad or rude or something, she could hardly look him in the eye.

"Is this all the luggage you have?" Hugh swung her rucksack on to his shoulder and picked up her holdall.

"Yes, travelling light." Janey pulled herself together.

Whatever reservations or suspicions she had about Hugh, they would have to work together. The least she could do was to be civil to him.

"Katie brings more than this for a weekend." Hugh smiled warmly at Janey.

"Yes that's sounds about right for Katie." Janey returned his smile. The mention of Katie and her notorious inability to travel with more than the kitchen sink broke the awkwardness Janey felt.

"The Land Rover's this way. I'll put your bags in then we could have a wee walk around the village if you like. Get you acquainted with the local landscape." Hugh walked towards the car park.

Janey followed, she'd rather have gone straight to Aigas, but said nothing. She'd rather have explored on her own, but to refuse would have been churlish. And she knew that if it had been John offering to show her round she'd have jumped at the chance. She'd have to try harder to trust her best friend's romantic choice. They walked up to the large main square. The main road ran through the middle and most of the shops were here. Hugh chatted easily, recounting the history of Beauly. They walked to the ruins of an old thirteenth century priory around which Beauly had grown. The ruins, made from the local red stone, had a peaceful air about them and although late in the year one or two people were sitting on benches enjoying the setting sun. They walked up to the large main square.

"It's quiet here now that the tourists have gone." Hugh broke the silence between them and sounded relaxed and friendly, which gave Janey hope that they could get rid of the tension between them.

"Yes, and the building is beautiful, especially in this light. It will be on my list of places to explore while I'm here. Most folk abandon me at places like this because I like to read all the information."

"Well there are plenty of places full of history around here to visit and I expect we have all the guide books you'd need back at Aigas."

"That's a good suggestion. Thank you, Hugh."

The light was fading.

"We'd better get back, it will soon be time for dinner." Hugh opened the door of the Land Rover for her.

"Thanks, Hugh, I enjoyed the walk, this really is a lovely little town."

"Next time we'll go to the pub. I'll introduce you to some of the locals."

"Now that sounds like fun." Janey had warmed to Hugh in spite of herself. She even questioned herself about her suspicions of him. She climbed into the vehicle and they started the journey. The sun was almost gone as they drove the twisty road to Aigas. As they drew near, the sweep of the road gave Janey another look at the magnificent hunting lodge, well-lit and welcoming. The drive was littered with leaves, their yellows, oranges and reds like a carpet to welcome her, shining in the headlights.

Hugh pulled up outside the front door. He got out and took Janey's luggage out of the boot. He waved to John and drove away. John was waiting to meet her.

"Good to see you Janey, welcome to the team. I hope your journey was good. I'll take you to your cabin. You'll be sharing with Lindsay. You'd have met her when you stayed with the girls I think. There's just the two of you in the cabin at the moment, it sleeps six so there's plenty of room."

"Thanks John, I think I remember Lindsay, she's been here a while hasn't she?"

"Yes, nearly two years. She'll show you around I'm sure. And she'll spend some time with you tomorrow – show you the Land Rover and cars so that you can get around independently when you need to. Tomorrow we'll be going to the market for veg and meat so you'll know what to get if you're there yourself. Dinner's in half an hour, just join us when you're ready."

"Thanks, John, I'm looking forward to it. Are there many guests here?"

"There's a group of a dozen who are here on a bird watching week. They're a good bunch, very friendly, so there's plenty of cooking for you. Lucy's looking forward to having another pair of hands to help."

They walked around to the back of the lodge and through a gate marked "Private". This was where the staff lived. Some of the cabins were empty; Janey supposed they would be full in the height of the season when extra staff were needed. Her cabin was warm and cosy. Janey dumped her rucksack and holdall in her room. She sat on the bed. Here I am, she thought. I really am here. This is home until Christmas. She couldn't believe her luck. A job at Aigas, and she got accommodation and all her meals. And really, Janey would have been happy to come on a voluntary basis, but John had insisted.

"You're a member of staff, Janey, one of the Aigas family, paid and treated the same as everyone else." She looked around the room. The wooden clad walls and lined curtains made her feel snug and safe. There were even fresh flowers on the table and a small television in the corner. There were books in the bookcase and one or two ornaments. She rummaged in her holdall and took out a picture frame. She smiled at the happy faces in the picture and gave it pride of place on top of the bookcase. My babies, she thought. Bloody big babies now, but I'm so proud of them all. Janey hoped they were a little bit proud of their mum. They'd all been really supportive of her after they got over the shock of her wanting to work up here.

She took up one of the fluffy white towels and went into the bathroom. We've even got our own bathroom, practically en-suite, she thought. There was no sign of Lindsay, so after a quick wash Janey headed for the house. The air was still, hardly a breeze, and the light of the lamp showed her the way. She breathed in the cool autumn air and felt comforted by the light of her favourite lamp. She had a good feeling about all of this. She was looking forward to working as part of a team. Her supermarket job seemed a million miles away, and she was glad. Janey smiled to herself. Life was good, and about to get better.

Chapter 35

She's a funny one, that Janey. Hugh glanced in his mirror as he drove down the leafy drive. All smiles with John, but Hugh had his misgivings. He'd been annoyed, no, more than annoyed when he heard she'd been taken on in the house. He'd been scared too. Not that he'd said anything. It wasn't his place. But it all seemed a bit suspicious. Janey had just a bit too much of a history mirroring his. But then, he thought as he drove the long road home, why would Janey tell him these things if she'd been sent to spy on him? Was someone trying to put the frighteners on him? But then, he thought as he drove the long road home, why? The unexpected had happened before. And there was another thing. He'd fallen for Katie, Janey's friend. Was she part of the set up? Trying to get close so she'd find out about him. Surely not. He was just being paranoid. Or was he? Stranger things have happened. It all seemed too much of a coincidence. He'd been on the brink of telling Katie everything the last time she'd been to see him. But he hardly knew her and trust was not in his nature. He'd have to wait a while, find out if he could really trust her. He'd thought at first it was just a bit of a dalliance and had surprised himself at the strength of feeling he had for her. He hadn't felt like this for years and in all the time he'd been married, despite his wife's problems, and the situation he found himself in now, he'd never strayed. But Katie was different. She brought out the tender side in him, quite unexpectedly. He supposed countless men found themselves in this situation, torn between two women. He'd never thought it would happen to him. What a bloody cliché, he shook his head at himself. He'd have to be very careful. Maybe it had been a mistake introducing Katie to all his friends. But most of them thought of him as single, so what was the harm. He'd been so careful to keep work and private lives apart, he hated anyone prying into his business. He had some hard thinking to do. Getting out of this muddle was going to be a wee bit tricky.

And here was this meddling woman, Janey, working in the big house. It was all too close for comfort. Janey had seemed startled when he'd picked her up at the station. As though she was uncomfortable to be with him. Did she know or even suspect something? She'd tried to cover it up, but he'd sensed her unease. That's why he'd suggested a walk around Beauly – to see if she dropped any hints. But it was clear that once she'd composed herself she was giving nothing away. And what was with the light luggage. Janey had travelled as though she was just away for a few days, not a couple of months. Maybe she was just going to stay long enough to find all she could about him and then she'd be gone. He felt quite nervous at the thought of Janey and Katie together on his home territory. Surely Katie wouldn't have set Janey up to spy on him.

The thought of Katie betraying him hurt far more than it should. But then he was keeping a secret from her. Would she feel betrayed when she found out? If she ever found out. He'd have to keep his distance from Janey. Make sure he gave nothing away when she was around. It shouldn't be too hard, with her working in the house and him on the estate most of the day with guests. The difficulty would be at mealtimes. It would be obvious to the whole team if he was avoiding her. They were such a close team, someone would notice.

Especially Lindsay, she noticed everything. She was a good listener, a good friend to him since she'd arrived and there had been several occasions of late when he'd nearly taken her into his confidence. But he knew people. You tell one, even in strictest confidence, believing them when they swear they'll tell no one, then before you know it, the secret's out and everyone has an opinion. That wouldn't do at all. Island life in Shetland had taught him that. He thought back to the time he'd "borrowed" his father's van to drive him and a mate to the pub about five miles from the croft. His dad had been out in the fields with the sheep. Hugh had known his dad would probably have given him permission, but he also knew he was expected to ask first. It was an old van, eaten through with rust on the passenger side floor so you could see the road. The memory made him smile as he drove home in his comfortable Land Rover with heated comfy seats and power steering – cars and vans suffered in Shetland with the salt spray from the sea. By the time he'd driven the single track road to the pub, no easy task with the numerous potholes and puddles of indeterminate depth, the landlord had informed them that Hugh's dad was looking for them – and the van. The pub did have a phone, but his dad had no mobile and there was no phone in the croft. How the jungle drums beat in the expanse of Shetland.

And now Lindsay was sharing a cabin with Janey. They'd become friends no doubt. Thank goodness he'd told Lindsay nothing.

And how would he cope when Katie came to stay again? Hugh knew he'd have to sort it out, but how. The sensible thing to do would have been to cool it with Katie, sort his private life and maybe then they'd have a chance. Christ, even the thought of not seeing Katie again made his heart clench. She'd really got to him. Part of him wished he'd explained to her right from the start. But she'd probably have had nothing to do with him. He knew Katie's ex-husband had cheated on her and she'd explained in no uncertain terms what she thought of cheating husbands. Way too late for that now, Katie would never understand. He'd just have to hope the situation at home would be solved soon and he could go to Katie with a clear conscience. He supposed his conscience would never be entirely clear, but maybe when he got his home life sorted and then explained, she'd at least give him a fair hearing. Who could ever second guess the reaction of a woman though? Certainly not a man with a secret.

Chapter 36

Janey was enjoying herself hugely. She'd started her first day at six thirty in the morning, making breakfast for the guests. She had her green Aigas polo shirt on and it bolstered her shrinking confidence at the tasks that lay ahead. She shouldn't have worried; the kitchen ran like clockwork and Janey fitted in just fine. Her cooking skills were much appreciated, and the team had a good laugh in the kitchen. Unlike some of the TV programmes, there was a lot of teamwork and no shouting. A recipe for success.

Fantastic porridge, Sir John assured everyone he'd made it himself, which brought a smile to Lady Lucy and the kitchen staff, Janey included. He had definitely stirred it himself, but the finer touches were down to Lucy. Well fed, the guests prepared to go on their morning walk. They all had the packed lunches the kitchen staff prepared earlier. Janey felt like a fish out of water, but the rest of them made her feel more than welcome. After the guests had gone, they all sat down for a bit of breakfast themselves.

"Right, now the rush is over, let's get cleared up." Lucy started clearing the plates and took them to the kitchen. "You start stacking the dishwasher, Janey. Just rinse the plates first."

"No problem, even I can do that." Janey laughed. "Just give me all the easy tasks till I get my bearings."

"We all muck in together and I can understand how you feel. But it won't be long before you know where everything is. Just ask as you go and you'll soon get your bearings."

Janey and Lucy cleared up, chatting easily. Janey was so pleased that Lucy was so easy-going and soon felt like they were old friends.

"There's no one in for lunch, so help yourself from the staff fridge. Lindsay should be around then too, so you can catch up with her. I'm sure you two will get on very well. Lindsay will appreciate the company."

Lucy showed Janey the fridge and where to get all she'd need. "I'll finish up in here, you can clean the tables and hoover the hall. I'll show you the cleaning cupboard. Then come back to the kitchen and we'll get prepared for dinner."

"The size of the hall, it'll take me till dinner time to hoover."

"Don't worry," Lucy smiled at her, "It won't take nearly as long as you think. Not with our industrial size vacuum."

Janey busied herself with cleaning the long tables. And Lucy had been right; the hoovering was much faster than she'd thought.

"I'm investing in one of those when I get home," Janey said to Lucy when she got back to the kitchen. "That's a fantastic machine."

"Well when you've got guests and a busy day, anything that makes the job easier is a bonus." Lucy was at the huge sink cleaning the vegetables. "But I know what you mean, it's so efficient. Listen to us Janey drooling over housework. Come and help with the veg and tell me a bit about yourself."

"Not much to tell really." Janey joined her and started scrubbing the potatoes. "I'm divorced with three children and looking for a bit of a change."

"This is a big change for you. Why did you want to work at Aigas?"

"I fell in love with it when we came for the weekend. There just seems to be something in the air. And you were so friendly."

"It must have been a big wrench to give up your job and head here, though. Usually our seasonal workers are students."

"I know, that's why I was so thrilled when John agreed to let me come. I know he took a bit of a chance me being older and not really the usual kind of worker."

"Not at all, he was delighted. Look at all the skills you have. You can cook, you know how a kitchen runs, you know how to use a hoover and you love it here. There was no question for him. With skills like you have, you'll be an asset to the team. It's hard to get anyone to work at this time of the year once the universities go back. I'm very grateful for another pair of hands."

"Well, I'm delighted to be here. I'll miss the children, but they're all grown up now, they've got their own lives to lead."

"I know what you mean, when our brood all come back, it's chaos, but I'm glad they're all getting on with their own lives too. I'm lucky to have Gordon, I think you met him when you were last here, he's the manager. He's our middle son and his wife, Sarah, is the local vet. They live in a house on the estate. He's good fun and easy to work with. We had no idea he'd want to come and work here after university but it's working very well. Sarah is on hand to help with our animals too which is great."

"It makes a big difference when you get on well with your kids." Janey felt a pang of longing as she said it. "I miss them all, we had such fun when they were growing up. But I'm lucky that they all get on well and don't see visiting me as a chore."

"Yes we have a lot to be thankful for." Lucy smiled her warm smile at Janey. "Come on, or we'll be crying into the veg with our motherly thoughts. Get the kettle on. We're nearly finished here. All I really have to do is put the roast in later and dinner will be ready. I made the chocolate mousse yesterday; all we have to do is wash some raspberries to go with it. Fancy some shortbread with your tea?"

"Only if it's your home-made shortbread. I'm trying to cut down on biscuits, but that is irresistible." Janey held out the cup to Lucy.

"Don't worry, Janey" Lucy said. "We'll work you so hard, the pounds will drop off."

"Great, I'll have another piece then."

They both laughed as they sipped their tea in the huge homely kitchen. The view from the window was stunning. Janey could see beyond the sweeping drive over to the wide valley. She could just make out the fast-flowing river as it cut its way through the bottom of the valley. Something caught her eye high above the trees.

"Is that a buzzard?"

"No, that's a golden eagle. We have a pair nesting on the estate." Lucy joined her at the window. "On a clear day like today they look magnificent. They're much bigger than a buzzard and the wing tip feathers fan out, see?" Lucy pointed to the huge bird in the distance.

"I saw them when we were here for the girly weekend, it's wonderful. What a lovely bonus on my first day."

"Take the binoculars and go to the big hide up from the house. It's only a few minutes' walk and you'll get a good view. Look, there's the other one; they'll be hunting. Be quick, the binoculars are behind the front door."

"Are you sure, don't you need help here?" Janey didn't want to take advantage of Lucy's good nature.

"I'm nearly done, you take your chance; they're flying closer. We're all used to stopping what we're doing if nature gives us a sight to see. Don't miss the chance or you'll regret it."

"Thanks Lucy." Janey called as she hurried out of the kitchen.

She picked up a pair of binoculars, grabbed her jacket, pulled on her boots and hurried up the path. She remembered the hide was at the edge of the pine wood. She climbed the tall wooden ladder onto the platform. Leaning on the wooden wall, she focussed the binoculars. There it was. And its mate not far away. The view was amazing. With the powerful binoculars she felt like she could reach out and touch the magnificent bird. She watched for a while, delighting in her good fortune.

Reluctantly, she climbed down from the hide as the birds glided away into the far distance. Lucy's words came to mind.

"Don't miss the chance or you'll regret it."

Janey was taking her chances and, so far, was regretting nothing.

Chapter 37

Janey got back and helped Lucy finish preparing for dinner that evening. She fixed some fresh ham and lettuce rolls and waited for Lindsay in the bright kitchen. She felt a bit nervous, Lindsay had been very friendly to her at dinner the night before, but she hadn't had much time to chat to her. It felt a bit strange sharing accommodation with someone almost young enough to be her daughter. Lindsay was one of the rangers, so Janey would get an insight into the work they did.

"Hey, hope you've got lunch ready, I'm starving. I saw Lucy in the drive and she said you'd be free for a natter." Lindsay took off her outdoor boots and called to Janey from the hall.

"Yes, all ready." Janey called back, "I'm in the kitchen."

"It's lovely and warm in here, it's getting chilly out in the moor." Lindsay sat down on the easy chair on the other side of the Aga. "I love this time of year with all the colours of the trees, but the winter's definitely on the way."

"I hope ham and lettuce is OK? I've made up some mayo with mustard but didn't know if you'd like some."

"That would be great, I'll help myself. Want some juice or tea or anything?"

"I'm sticking to the mineral water, I've had enough tea so far today." Janey loved the enthusiasm Lindsay always had, she'd been good fun on the girly weekend.

"How's your first day been so far, broken any dishes yet?"

"Not so far, the time's going fast, so I reckon I'm enjoying it. Sorry I went straight to bed last night, I was exhausted with all the excitement. All this fresh highland air certainly makes me sleep well."

"I was the same when I came, I've never slept so soundly in my life. I love it here, it's like a second home." Lindsay took a bite of her roll. "This is good, it's going to be great having another good cook around."

"It's only a roll, I've had plenty of practice over the years with picnics for the kids."

"Sounds like fun, I used to love picnics as a kid. How many have you got?"

"Three; boy, girl, boy. They're all doing their own thing now though, all in their twenties."

"Jeez, you don't look old enough. Child bride, were you?"

"Almost, and it was hard work having three so close together, but it's good now, they all feel like friends. We're a good team – me and the kids. I've been a single parent for a long time. And better for it I think."

"Yep, that's common nowadays, my folks split up when I was in my teens. Should have done it long before, but they did that staying together for the sake of my big sister and me. Hey, any more rolls?"

"Yes, there's more in the fridge. I didn't know how hungry you'd be after all that fresh air."

"Yes, I do get hungry; the hard work gives me an appetite." Lindsay uncurled herself from the chair and headed for the fridge. "Want one?"

"No, I'm fine. Watching the diet."

"You don't look like you need to." Lindsay curled back on the chair with another roll and a top up of tea.

"Oh, if you'd seen me a couple of months ago, you'd not have said that." Janey pulled her stomach in unconsciously. "I had to get a bit of weight off and it's going really well. I've been doing far more exercise too and it all helps. I needed to get myself fit to come up here or I'd never have managed the hills."

The two women laughed, then Janey remembered. "I saw the golden eagles this morning, Lucy sent me up to the hide to get a better view, they're magnificent."

"You're lucky, it was weeks before I got my first glimpse. They're something else though. Makes you proud to be

Scottish. We're very lucky to have a pair nesting so close to the house."

"I could have watched them all day," Janey nodded. "It's going to be a real bonus having all this wildlife around."

"That's what makes working here so special. Have you seen the beavers yet? John got permission last year to manage a release of them. He's the real expert."

"No, I've not seen them yet, would John let me? I thought they were a closely guarded secret."

"Oh not so much now, not now that they seem to be established. But John wants them to get really settled before he adds them to the bigger tourist trail. He'd be delighted to share his little project. If he's not around, ask Hugh."

"I'm not sure Hugh really likes me. I just seem to get a conversation going and then he backs off. It's awkward with him seeing my friend Katie."

"Ah, the new girlfriend. Don't worry about Hugh, I've known him a long time but I hardly know anything about him if you know what I mean. I was even surprised to find out he was seeing someone. He's never had a romantic entanglement in all the time I've known him. Though he'd probably keep it a secret, he's a deep one." Lindsay poured herself more tea. "He even stays in his own bothy away from Aigas. I've never been there and haven't a clue where it is. He doesn't really say much about himself. But he's good to work with and knows his stuff. And the ladies love him. I'm glad he's found Katie. I often think he looks quite lonely."

"Oh well, maybe it's not just me then." Janey was relieved with what Lindsay said, but chose not to share what she'd learned in Majorca. It would seem like gossip and she didn't want to seem like she was nosey. Not when they were just getting to know each other. "I'll just have to make allowances and respect his privacy."

"Best way. I had quite a fancy for him when I first came. Tried like mad to get to know him better, but he's the master of getting you to talk about yourself and giving nothing away to do with him."

Janey thought of what Katie had said about Hugh. "I think Katie feels the same, but she's head over heels about him. I think she's coming up next weekend to see him."

"Well, she got further than I did." Lindsay laughed. "I don't think he took kindly to my constant questions. But then I'm just a nosey cow. It's been my downfall in many a relationship."

Janey laughed with her. "I'd better get on; I've beds to make up before the guests get back. No rest for the wicked."

"No indeed, and I've got to swot up on tomorrow's bird watch, catch you later." Lindsay stood up and headed for the library.

Janey went through to the back door and put on her boots. She shrugged her jacket around her shoulders and went out into the cold afternoon air.

As she trudged to the first of the guest cabins her thoughts turned to the dark highlander. Maybe being secretive was just his nature. Maybe he preferred to keep his past there. But it troubled Janey that he'd never mentioned a wife, or hopefully ex-wife to Katie. She was still in a dilemma about whether to tell Katie what she'd accidentally learned in Majorca, but she didn't want to cause a row with Katie, or annoy Hugh, and she certainly didn't want to jeopardise her work at Aigas. Maybe she should take Lindsay's advice and not let being a nosey cow and spoil anything.

Janey opened the door of the first cabin. She pushed the uncomfortable thoughts from her mind. These beds wouldn't make themselves.

Chapter 38

Janey hardly had time to think that first week. She was already able to help with the cooking for big numbers, something she had only ever had to do at Christmas, when the whole family came to her house. The time seemed to fly and although the work was pretty constant there was always the chance to see some of the estate. She'd asked John at dinner one evening about the beavers.

"You'll love them," he enthused. "We got our first lot last year and they're settling in well. I'd be delighted to show you if you've got the time. That is if my wife isn't working you too hard." He smiled at Lucy who caught his look and smiled back.

"There's always time for outdoors in this job. It's a pleasure to have Janey so interested in everything. And a real bonus that she's such a good cook."

Janey smiled too, hugely encouraged by Lucy's words. She knew she was a good cook but had found the number of people she was helping cook for quite daunting at first. Lucy was a superb cook and Janey was learning quickly from her end enjoying it enormously.

"I'd love to see the beavers," she told John. "Did you have any trouble with local folk when you got permission to re-introduce them to the wild?"

"Some," John answered. "But most folk are quite supportive when they understand the benefits to the environment. And eventually as the numbers grow they'll be quite an attraction. A bit like the ospreys at Loch Garten. We have to keep the beaver's exact location a secret at the moment to help them establish, but I'd be happy to take you. They'll be a real investment to the highland wildlife community eventually."

"Speaking of investing; and changing the subject. I need some financial guidance about a recent inheritance and wondered if there's anyone local that could help. Do you know of anyone?" Janey paused while John thought.

"What about David, John," Lucy offered.

"Of course, David. He's a good friend of ours now, Janey, but he's an independent advisor and he's served us well over the years. He's got a business in Inverness but he'd be happy to come and see you here."

"Hasn't he recently opened a wee office in Beauly?" Lucy asked.

"You're quite right, what would I do without you to organise me and remember things." John and Lucy exchanged smiles.

"You'd like David," said John "he's very honest about the advice he gives. He has a junior partner who's a woman if you'd prefer the fairer sex advising you."

"No, David sounds just fine. I'll get his number from you and give him a call. All I've done so far is left the money in a high interest account in the bank, but my aunt's lawyer did advise me to talk to someone."

"David's quite friendly with Hugh and they sometimes meet up for a drink at the pub in Beauly on a Friday. Ask Hugh to take you in and introduce you. An informal meeting will give you the chance to chat." John pushed back his chair and looked towards the guests further down the table. "I'm taking this lot to the pine martin and badger hide this evening, I should see Hugh there, I'll mention it."

"Thanks, John I'd appreciate it."

Janey wasn't sure if Hugh would appreciate being lumbered with her. She'd spoken to him a few times but got the distinct impression he was reluctant to engage her in conversation. She'd had no chance to really chat and broach the subject of his personal life. Still, Katie was coming up at the weekend, maybe she'd know more after that. Lindsay hadn't really told her anything else either. Not that she'd been trying to pry, but after every aborted conversation with Hugh, she still had the feeling he was hiding something.

She got the opportunity to catch Hugh at breakfast the next day. She waited until he sat down then casually sat beside him. He didn't look up.

"Hi there, how's it going?" A feeble start, but his lack of greeting made Janey feel awkward.

"Fine. Busy."

"John told me you know a financial guy in Inverness. David I think he said."

"Yes, he mentioned you needed some advice." Hugh ventured no more so Janey tried again.

"John said you met him on Fridays sometimes. Any chance I could tag along with you to meet him?"

Hugh looked up and seemed to put on a forced smile. "Sure, I'm meeting Katie from the train at Beauly this Friday and we're meeting up with a couple of folk after we've eaten and David should be at the pub. I'll give you a lift if you like."

"Yes, Katie mentioned she was coming up when we spoke on the phone, and no need for a lift, I'll borrow one of the estate's cars and meet you there if you give me directions. Don't want to be a gooseberry with you lovebirds."

Hugh returned her smile with a shadow of a frown, but he looked relieved. "It's the Lovat Arms Hotel. The public bar. You can't miss it, it's on the main street."

"I think I remember from the tour you gave me when I arrived, thanks. Eight o'clock be OK?"

"Should be fine. Must get on." Hugh left the table and headed for the group he was taking that day.

He's a really odd guy, Janey thought. I wonder what Katie sees in him sometimes. She sings his praises, but all I seem to get is the cold shoulder. I wish he'd make more of an effort, especially when he's seeing my best friend. Of course maybe deep and meaningful conversation was less important than the sweet loving Katie was getting. She was glad she'd turned down the offer of a lift. The drive to Beauly would have been difficult if it was a one-way conversation, and she didn't fancy hanging around or going for a meal with them. She'd catch up with Katie at the pub. The thought made Janey smile. She was looking forward to seeing Katie. And when she'd called Fraser, he said he was hoping to be in Beauly the next day. He was camping with friends in Inverness. All the new friends she'd made here were great but seeing an old friend, and her son, would be better.

She started collecting the dishes. She'd have to ask Lucy if there was a car she could borrow otherwise she'd have to grovel to Hugh and ask him for a lift after all. And she guessed she'd be getting a cab back in that case. She couldn't imagine Hugh offering to take her home with Katie desperate to drag him off to bed. No, borrowing a car was the best plan. And if she wasn't drinking she could keep her wits about her for any clues about Hugh. Although she'd have to remember why she was going. Financial advice from David – not playing amateur detective.

Chapter 39

Katie was very glad she'd booked her seat. The train was busy. She supposed it was because it was Friday. Katie sat facing the direction of her journey. She couldn't wait to see Hugh. The week had seemed to drag even though they'd talked nearly every day. And now she'd have three whole days with him. The thought of him taking her in his arms and kissing her made her insides melt with delight. She smiled to herself, she was behaving like a lovesick teenager, but she loved it. It was a glorious feeling, the first flush of romance, made her feel young again. Not that she was that old, but fifty was just around the corner. She was glad the passenger opposite her across the table seemed engrossed in their book, she didn't feel like making small talk with a stranger today. She just wanted to enjoy the journey and the fabulous scenery and dream about the weekend ahead, and Hugh. It would be getting dark by the time she got to Inverness and the fading light as she travelled gave another dimension to the forests and moors she passed. And of course she was looking forward to seeing Janey. They'd talked that morning.

"I'm really glad to be coming up to see you."

"Nonsense, it's not me you're coming to see, it's Hugh." Janey had chuckled to her friend. "If he wasn't here, you'd never have come to stay."

"Rubbish." Katie replied indignantly. "Of course I would have come up, you're my friend and I miss you. Besides, I'm looking forward to a cosy chat over a glass of wine, speaking on the phone's not the same."

"The only person you want to get cosy with is Hugh and you know it. I'll be lucky to get five minutes with you."

"Well, you'll get longer than that on Saturday, Hugh's working during the day so you and I can explore Beauly."

"Ah, second best now, and you'll spend the entire time drooling over Hugh and watching the clock until it's time to meet him. I know you."

It was Katie's turn to laugh, "You know me so well. I promise not to go on about him too much. I can't risk losing my best friend now, can I? Anyway, you get him all the time; I can only visit every couple of weeks. How are you two getting along anyway?"

"Well, to be honest," Katie heard the hesitation in her friend's voice, "I hardly see him really with working in the house and he's outside mostly. Even in the evenings once all the work's done he doesn't hang around like the others, just goes home. Keeps himself to himself mostly."

"Yes he's not one for chatting I suppose. More a man of action." Katie had laughed with Janey at the suggested innuendo.

"Nothing wrong with that, especially since you've been in the desert sex-wise for so long. I just hope your good luck rubs off on me soon. I could do with a bit of physical dalliance."

"Well you're not exactly going to find a man cooped up in the highlands. We'll have to work on you when you get home at Christmas. Will I see you this evening when I get there?"

"Yes, I'm borrowing Lucy's car and coming to Beauly around eight. Hugh's going to introduce me to David, his financial buddy, so I can get some advice about the money."

"You'll like David; I met him last time I was up. A bit too slick for my tastes, but a good laugh. Betty will be there too probably, have you met her?"

"From the book shop? Yes, I've spoken to her a few times, her shop is a real treasure trove. I love it. I still feel like giggling whenever I see the shop "Betty's Books" I was sure her name was made up."

"I know, I was the same, but it really is her name. She's known Hugh a long time I think."

"God, any excuse to bring his name into the conversation." Janey laughed.

"OK, OK, I get the hint, anyway, see you soon." Katie smiled as she remembered the conversation. Janey was a good friend to her, and much as she was desperate to see Hugh, she was very much looking forward to catching up with Janey. If the weather held, they could pack a picnic tomorrow and she'd get Janey to show her some of the estate, Janey had arranged to get the day off. Katie began to dose as the train hurried north. She'd better grab some sleep now, with any luck she'd get precious little for the next two nights.

Chapter 40

Janey felt quite nervous as she parked the car. She looked around the town square. The night was crisp and dark. She dug her hands deep into her pockets, glad of the warmth of her coat. She looked up. The stars are wonderful at this time of year, especially when the night is as clear as this, she thought, and the lights on in the houses gave a cheery light all around her. I'm looking forward to seeing Katie, if she has the time to chat when Hugh's around, Janey smiled to herself. She crossed the road and went into the lounge bar of the Lovat Arms. God, I hope there's someone there I know. She felt silly to be nervous but it was different going in to a new place by herself. She'd left it till just past eight o'clock in the hope that Katie and Hugh would have arrived ahead of her. The lights in the welcoming bar were bright in contrast to the dark outside.

Janey unbuttoned her coat as she stood in the doorway letting her eyes adjust to the brightness. She scanned the bar. No familiar faces. Then she heard Katie's laugh. That's a relief, she's here, Janey sighed, her fear melting away. She followed the laughter to the back of the bar. Katie was sitting with three others including Hugh. Janey recognised Betty from the bookshop. She'd chatted to her when she'd gone into Beauly to top up on her reading. But she hadn't met her socially, and Janey was looking forward to that. She didn't know the other man, but Janey guessed it would be David, the financial guy.

"Hey, starting without me." Janey shrugged off her coat as she greeted the group.

"Hi, there." Katie stood up and hugged Janey. "Can't hang around for latecomers, there's drinking to do. It's so good to see you, Janey, how's the work going. They're obviously working you far too hard. You're fading away to a shadow."

Janey grinned at her friend as she returned the hug. Katie was good. She knew how sensitive Janey was about her weight. "Work is really good, I feel more like I'm in an extended holiday sometimes, and the food's excellent so it's tempting to stuff myself. Luckily this highland air seems to encourage walking, so I'm getting fitter all the time."

"You look great anyway, come on, sit down and I'll introduce you."

Janey sat on the seat they'd saved for her. The bar was busy being a Friday evening. They were seated around a low table at the best seats in the house. Beside them the heat from the crackling log fire warmed her.

"This is David." Katie sneaked a knowing wink at Janey.

Janey caught the look and held her hand out to the man sat beside her. "Pleased to meet you. Hugh mentioned you'd be here. I'm Janey."

"Great to meet you too." David took her hand and kissed the back of it. "Always glad to have a pretty girl in the company."

Janey retrieved her hand, annoyed that she could feel her face go pink. Katie and Betty squealed their protest.

"Excuse me," Betty started, "what about the other 'pretty girls' in the company?" Katie nodded in agreement.

"Ah, you two are taken, what I meant was its good to have a single pretty girl in the company."

"And just how did you know I'm single?" It was Janey's turn to shoot a knowing look in Katie's direction. Katie didn't even have the temerity to blush.

"I told him. It's about time you had a little romance in your life." Katie's eyes twinkled.

"So what's this, a blind date with an audience?" Janey tried to sound injured, but the others were enjoying the fun.

"Certainly not, just a few friends gathering for a blether. How could you think I'd set you up?"

"Katie, when you're loved up you expect everyone to be looking for a lover."

It was Katie's turn to blush, and she turned to Hugh. "Save me from my friend."

"Not a chance, you should leave her alone to sort out her own love life." Hugh was smiling at Janey, the first time since she'd started working at Aigas that he'd spoken to her properly.

"Now that that's sorted, let's get another round in. What would you like, Janey?"

Janey looked at David, noticing his clear blue eyes and eyelashes she'd die for. "Just a soda water and lime thanks, I'm driving."

Janey knew she sounded less than friendly, but something about David got her back up. From the hand kissing and the forced flattery, not to mention being referred to as a "girl", made her think he was a wee bit too cheesy for her liking. Janey wasn't at all sure she'd want to meet him on a one to one.

Turning on the charm was all good and well, but Janey preferred to be comfortable around folk she was trusting with her money. Anyway, tonight was about good company, she could keep the business till later. She watched as the others chatted easily. She felt a little bit left out. They all seemed so relaxed and Katie had clearly been included into the group. She felt a little stab of jealousy. Katie was her friend. This is ridiculous, she chided herself. I'm a grown woman, not some daft teenager. I'm pleased Katie's having a good time and she and Hugh seemed very happy. I should be glad at the way things have worked out. But Janey couldn't help feeling a bit uneasy. Katie hadn't mentioned anything about Hugh being married. Even if he had an ex-wife, Janey was sure Katie would have mentioned it. Surely that would have given them some common ground. Of course, it was none of Janey's business. They were both gown women, capable of looking after themselves. But Janey still wanted to look out for her friend. The way she hoped Katie would look out for her if she was in an awkward situation. Janey really didn't know if she should say anything or let it be. If she told Katie what she'd found out about Hugh when she was in Majorca, Katie might be mad at her for not saying something sooner. On the other hand, if Janey said nothing and it came out later that Janey had had her suspicions - and he really was married - Katie would never speak to her again. But surely, she thought, Hugh's friends wouldn't be so welcoming of Katie if Hugh had a wife? They must know his circumstances. Betty had known Hugh since university. Surely she wouldn't condone Hugh behaving like that? But Janey knew people. Nothing would surprise her.

"Penny for them?" David turned to Janey. "You're lost in your thoughts. Fancy sharing them."

Janey smiled at him, blushing. She'd been miles away, not even listening to the conversation. "Sorry, busy day at work. I'm not used to socialising here, you must think me very rude."

"The ruder the better," David said with a wink, "I like a girl with an imagination."

Janey was not sure how to take him, or how to reply. She looked at him. Charming certainly, with a lovely smile and come to bed eyes, which she was sure could turn many a woman's heart. But she did object to being referred to as a girl. There was something in his tone that conveyed an undercurrent of sensuality and she didn't find it attractive at all. He was good looking though, she had to admit. Well cut light ginger hair, greying at the sides and a cheeky dimple when he smiled.

"Oh, I can be imaginative when I want," she parried back, lifting her head and giving him her most charming smile, "for a woman."

"Ah, point taken, not a girl, a woman. I stand corrected and suitably put down." David hung his head in mock shame and looked for all the world like a naughty school boy.

Janey had to laugh along with the others. She felt herself relax, as long as he knew where he stood and that she wasn't someone who'd fall at his feet, she'd be OK.

"Good to see you've made her smile and got her back here with us," Katie quipped, "I thought for a minute our conversation was boring her, well done Dave."

"Sorry guys, just a lot on my mind, ignore me." Janey took a big breath, tried to forget her worries about Hugh, and join in.

"I was asking if any of you had been to the Edinburgh Book Festival," Betty was saying. "I know Janey's a bookworm, she's been in the shop a few times."

"And I was saying if it wasn't for the Book Festival, I'd never have met Hugh. And you would never have ended up here working, Janey. Some things are just meant to be." Katie glanced at Hugh and they shared look that none of the others were included in.

"How come?" said David "You've not told me this story, Hugh. I'd no idea you were 'booky' enough to go the Book Festival."

Hugh smiled his lazy smile. "Och' well, there's a lot even you don't know about me Dave."

Janey felt the smile on her face freeze. None of the others seemed the least bit bothered at this statement from Hugh and just laughed. Hugh said no more, so Katie continued, clearly delighted to enlighten David about her budding romance with Hugh.

"He's not been there; it was when I went in August and heard John talking about Aigas. I was entranced with the talk, he made it sound so magical quite apart from the work he was doing there, and I thought it would be the perfect for the girls for a weekend."

David interrupted her, "So it's OK for you to refer to your pals as girls, but not for me when I'm only doing my best to offer compliments."

Katie grinned. "When you put it like that, I see your point, do accept our humble apologies."

Even Janey had to concede he had a point. I guess we can all be hypocritical she thought, thinking of her problem with Hugh. We can all say one thing and do another. Katie continued with her story and brought Janey back to the conversation.

"Anyway, we decided to come up here, although Janey wasn't coming at first, then when she got…" Katie stopped and looked at Janey, clearly not wanting to talk about her new financial situation.

"It's OK, Katie, Betty and Hugh can both know and I'm hoping David will give me some professional advice." Janey turned to David. "What Katie means is that I got a small inheritance, which meant I could pack in my crap job and go and do something I really wanted to do. For myself. So I'd like to pick you brains about a wee bit of investment sometime."

"Leave the financial chat to later, you two." Katie didn't give David a chance to answer Janey. Katie had centre stage and she wasn't going to relinquish it until she'd told her tale.

"Well, Janey could come after all, and as walking and nature is her "thing" she was looking forward to it. She even told me she was looking for a dark highlander, but I nabbed him first."

"Excuse me, that's not exactly how it happened, I was not man-hunting. Well, not nearly as much as you." Janey was laughingly indignant while Hugh was starting to look a bit uncomfortable.

"Well, the best girl won, sorry David, the best woman." Katie looked adoringly at Hugh who only just managed to hold her gaze.

"You dark horse Hugh," David exclaimed. "I did keep asking him how you two met, but never got a straight answer. Dark Highlander indeed, that's a good nickname."

"Only he's not from the highlands," Betty chipped in, "He's from Shetland."

"No matter," David replied, "Dark Highlander it is from now on."

"Don't tease, you've touched a nerve there, clearly." Katie sensed Hugh's discomfort. Janey did too.

"Definitely," Betty nodded, "you know our Hugh, never likes to be in the spotlight or reveal anything about himself. I've known him forever and he can still surprise me."

"Get away you lot, can a man not enjoy his pint in peace without all this blethering," Hugh tried to sound light-hearted.

"We'll need to change the subject or he'll get all huffy." Betty smiled at Hugh and Janey thought she caught a cautious look pass between them. Katie and David hadn't noticed. Maybe Janey was being too sensitive. "So will you be at the Book Festival next year?" Betty asked Katie and Janey.

"I will be, now that I have more time. It's been hard to get to events with working at the supermarket. The festival's such a busy time in Edinburgh and I've usually had to do extra shifts. Thank God I'll not have to do that any more." Janey said with feeling. "In fact, I'd love to get involved with the Book Festival. Of all the festivals going on in Edinburgh, I think it's my favourite. Maybe I could do some voluntary work there?"

"You'd have to get a paid job there Janey." Katie laughed. "Enough to cover your book bill otherwise you'll blow your entire inheritance on books. Once you're let loose on their bookshop, we'll never see you again."

"I know that feeling," agreed Betty, "I often go down to see some of the Scottish authors there, and it's just such a good place to get all the latest titles for the shop. If I'm lucky I can come back with a few copies signed by the authors I've taken with me from here. There's always a surge in business when I get back from the Book Festival."

"Looks like I'm going to have to invest your cash wisely to cover your wild spending habits, Janey," David teased, "For most women it's shoes and handbags, sounds like your weakness is books."

"Not just mine, Katie's too. We swap all the time and raid the charity shops, then give them all back when we're done.

Mind you, if I collect any more books I'll be needing to move house. Between us, Katie and I could furnish a small library."

Katie nodded in agreement. "Janey will have read most of the books in your shop by the time she leaves here."

Betty agreed, "She's a good customer, I'll miss her. I'll just have to branch out in to mail order."

"That would be perfect," Janey agreed, "just let me know and I'll be your first customer." Janey felt better now that the conversation was on familiar ground. "My son, Fraser is coming for the day tomorrow, he's with friends in Inverness for a few days and he's as much of a book worm as I am, we'll need to pay you a visit."

"It would be lovely to meet him Janey. I'll look forward to it."

The chat drifted on, then she sensed Katie and Hugh were ready to leave.

"Early night for us I think." Katie got up to leave, not in the slightest bit worried that it was clear she was desperate to drag Hugh off to bed. Not that Hugh looked like he'd need to be dragged, Janey thought. The two of them were clearly lost in one another.

"Away you go lovebirds." David waved his hand at them. "You'll be rotten company if you keep on lusting after one another any more. Go get a room."

"I'll see you tomorrow, Janey, lunch at the bookshop café?" Katie shrugged her coat on with Hugh's help.

"Sure you'll be up by then? I mean out of bed by then?" They all laughed at Janey's unintended innuendo.

"I'll call you if I'm not." Katie looked at Hugh. "Maybe I'll be able to convince this hunk to stay all night for a change."

Janey caught another brief glance between Betty and Hugh. What was all that about, she thought. That was the second time, surely she wasn't imagining these stolen glances.

She could hardly concentrate on the conversation after Katie and Hugh left, and barely blinked when she found herself agreeing to meet David for a bar supper the next night to chat about her money.

She left the pub after saying her goodnights and promising to meet David.

Was she really sure she should be meeting him for something to eat, she pondered as she walked to the car, it seemed more of a date rather than a formal discussion about investing her money. She should have been thinking faster and made an appointment at his office the following week. She didn't want him to get the idea that she fancied him or anything. He was nice enough but a bit too smooth for her liking. That naughty twinkle in his eye spelt danger, and heartache. Anyway, he just didn't do it for her, she thought as she turned out of Beauly and onto the Aigas road, not so much as a twinkle for all his cheeky charm. She might be able to get more information about Hugh though. But from what his friends seemed to think, he was a closed book. She laughed to herself. Considering the topic of conversation for most of the evening, that was a pretty funny comment for her. Closed book indeed.

Chapter 41

They strolled hand in hand from the pub to the bed and breakfast where Katie was staying above Betty's shop. It was a crisp starlit night and Katie was feeling lovely. She'd had a good time at the pub and, although Janey had seemed unusually preoccupied from time to time, she thought it had all gone well. It was a good feeling when the man in her life was happy to introduce her to all his friends and make her feel so welcome. His hand felt good, she squeezed it and he gave her a squeeze back and a deep look, which left her in no doubt about his intentions when they got back to her room. She'd hoped Janey would have been a bit more chatty with David, with his outgoing personality and good humour, although he wasn't to Katie's taste, a bit of romance might be good for Janey. But she could tell Janey hadn't been that impressed with him. Maybe if she met with him to discuss money, he'd work his charm. Katie daydreamed as she walked with Hugh about her and Janey travelling up on the train to meet their men in the months to come. Janey was only working at Aigas till Christmas, but there was plenty time for her and David to get together.

"What are you plotting?" Hugh broke into her thoughts.

"Nothing, just thinking."

"That's a plotting expression you've got there. I can tell. Scheming about getting David and Janey together perhaps?"

"Of course not, that's their business. Nothing at all to do with me." Katie tried and failed to sound indignant.

"Sure," Hugh smiled at her, "I think David seemed keen, I've not seen him try so hard around a woman for a long while, but I'm not sure Janey fell for his wit and charm."

"Well, yes," Katie conceded, "Janey seemed a bit distant tonight. I'll get a good gossip with her tomorrow and sing David's praises."

"Not too loud, you might scare her off. But he's a good bloke at heart. Not really found anyone since his marriage failed. I'd like to see him happy again."

"What happened?"

"Oh, he was better off out of it. His wife was a difficult type. Completely controlling. One of those that expected him to work night and day while she spent her days at the gym, out for lunch and spending all his cash where she pleased. David used to say she always put her family before him. He never got a look in, he was just expected to fill the bank account faster than she could spend it."

"Has he any children, he never mentions any?"

"No, thank goodness, she'd have made a terrible mother, always put herself first, children would have upset her lifestyle too much. I think he'd have liked kids though, just not with her."

"Well Janey's got three, but I'm not sure she'd have another one."

"Oh I think David feels a bit too old to start the nappy run. He'd settle for a good life partner I think."

"And what about you, Hugh, are you ready to settle for a good life partner?" Katie knew she was chancing her luck, they'd never really talked about the future, but she was in this for the long haul. She knew it. Maybe it was too soon to ask the question and she wasn't sure if she'd like the answer. Hugh was very cautious when it came to talking about personal things. Sometimes she even thought he deliberately avoided talking about himself. But she'd got him talking now, so she'd take her chance on his response. Hugh was silent and Katie wondered if she'd overstepped the mark.

"Well, that's a question." Hugh paused. "I like the way we're going, Katie. I don't want to spoil it. I like the way you don't pester me with questions all the time, and I must admit, you're the best lover I've ever had."

He reached for her and kissed her long and hard. She felt the passion rising in her, and as she responded, so did he.

"Lucky we're nearly at the room." He murmured in her ear. "Any further away and I'd have to take you out of sight and ravish you anyway, even in this cold."

Katie wasn't sure he'd really answered her question, but she wasn't going to spoil the moment. If they carried on like this there would be plenty time to look to the future.

She put the key in the lock and they climbed the stairs to her room. Inside was warm and cosy with a fire burning cheerfully, giving the room a sensual glow. Katie lit the candles on the mantelpiece.

"Don't put the lights on; I want to make love to you in front of the fire."

Hugh was undressing and helping her out of her clothes with a fierce urgency. Katie could have cried with love for him. But that was a word she'd never use first. This was a man she'd have to wait for. She just sensed it. He'd love her with all the physical passion he could but she'd have to wait for the rest. That didn't come easy for Katie. She liked to know exactly where she stood. But her lust for Hugh quickly overruled her head and they were soon entwined in front of the fire with Hugh reaching for all the deep places she'd grown to love him to touch. After their first flush of passion, Hugh carried Katie to the bed. The landlady had put a hot bottle in for her so the bed was cosy. Hugh held her in his arms and she could feel herself beginning to drift off to sleep, safe and satiated. "You'll stay tonight, won't you? Janey said you were off tomorrow." Katie was suddenly wide awake but didn't move. She'd felt him tense as she spoke.

"I can't. Janey wouldn't have known I'm covering for someone tomorrow. I have to be up early, so I'll go soon so I can get ready for the morning."

She shifted round so she could see him more clearly. She knew any comment could spoil the moment, but she couldn't help herself. She also knew she sounded like a whingeing child. "But you never stay. It would be so special. I feel empty when you go sneaking off in the early hours. I don't like waking up without you."

Hugh pulled her back against him. "Soon, I promise, I just have to take any extra shifts I can. I've got to save hard for some Edinburgh visits you know. Think how special it will be then. You'll have me all to yourself at home. Much better than here."

"But I like being here with you. This room is special. I just wish you could stay. It seems like every weekend I'm here you do extra work instead of taking time off."

"It'll be better soon, I promise." Hugh turned around so his face was touching hers. "You're very special to me, Katie. I know I'm not good at saying it but I'm not going for a while so let me show you how special you are."

Katie could feel his hardness pressing on her urgently. She responded immediately to him. Why waste the moment, she thought, there would be plenty time to spend whole nights together in the future. She'd have to be patient, but for the time being she could just lose herself in the passion.

Chapter 42

Hugh felt bad as he drove home. He hated leaving Katie all snuggled up in bed as he headed off in the dark and cold of night to his bothy. He'd never felt like this before about anyone, and had come close to throwing caution to the wind and telling Katie everything, again. He knew he should be straight with, her but for the time being it was best as few folk as possible knew. He knew he was falling in love with Katie, and hated himself for avoiding the truth when he was with her. He hadn't meant it to happen. In fact he'd kept so much to himself since being at Aigas that he knew he had a reputation for being unsociable. Especially by his colleagues. Not staying on site meant he missed the after work chat and occasional impromptu parties. But he had no choice. No, that was wrong as well, he had a choice. But not one he could exercise at the moment. He would really have to do some deep thinking and, when the time came, things would be easier. He knew being with Katie felt right and he knew this could be a deep and lasting love, yet his head kept telling him to stop. Not risk hurting her, and his family.

His family. He was risking everything at the moment on a reckless love affair. How would they react when it all came out? And it would. Eventually. He had to hope that until he sorted out the mess he was getting into, Isabel and the kids wouldn't find out. They never strayed far from the bothy, Isabel hating crowds of people. She wasn't easy to live with, and he knew how suspicious she was when he stayed out later than she liked. She'd already begun asking why he seemed to be doing very late shifts every other weekend and it wasn't even the height of the holiday season. He hated lying to her. He tried to convince himself it was to protect her. And in some ways, it was. His wee Isabel, and the kids. It would all come to a head, he knew that and he wasn't looking forward to it. David had told him once that the worst time was the weeks or months before a relationship break, that once the decision was made, life got easier. Hugh hoped David was right. He wasn't sure how long he could cope with the deception. He'd run away once before, to Majorca, and coming home to face the music had been brutal. But he'd survived it once, so he guessed he could do it again. He hoped Isabel and Katie would forgive him. But his future was with Katie, pray to God she'd understand. Eventually.

Hugh drove round the curve of the one-track road and saw the light on outside the bothy. He hoped Isabel was asleep. He didn't fancy answering any awkward questions.

He parked the Land Rover and let himself in to his house. There was no noise except the ticking of his granny's clock in the kitchen. He'd sleep on the couch again rather than risk waking Isabel or the kids. The answers he knew he'd have to give could wait till morning.

His main concern was Katie's reaction when she found out the truth. He really didn't want to lose her; his feelings were so strong. But what would her reaction be when she found out what was really going on.

Chapter 43

The wind had picked up and John had warned Janey as she left Aigas to go to Beauly that morning to watch the weather.

"If this storm sets in as promised, the road can flood, or if it's snow it could block with the drifts, so give yourself time to get back." John was serious in his concern for Janey.

"No problem, John, I'm meeting my son from the train this morning, but I expect he'll want to have a wander round Beauly at some point. I'm meeting Katie for lunch which I expect Fraser will avoid as he won't want to listen to our chatter and said to David I'd meet him for supper to talk about my money, but that could wait until next week if the weather is too bad. Fraser is getting the train about six, back to Inverness."

"Meeting the bold David indeed, worked his charm already has he?" John smiled knowingly. "Keep your eye on that one – he's an eye for the ladies."

"This is strictly business, I'm afraid I'm too long in the tooth to take his brand of charm seriously. Sound financial advice is all I need."

"Well, you'll certainly get that. Don't get me wrong, he's a sound bloke, but not really the settling down type if you know what I mean."

"The only settling down I intend to do I the near future is with a large whisky and a cup of cocoa. Anyway, I'll not be risking any storm for a bar supper with Mr Charmer."

"Good for you, see you later, take care on the road." John turned to go into the house. He was preparing a talk on winter birds in the highlands.

Janey was looking forward to seeing Fraser. She got to the small station in Beauly just in time for the train pulling in. One or two passengers got off and then she spotted Fraser moving slowly towards her. She rushed to give him a hug, but he flinched away from her. He looked pale.

"Careful Mum, I'm in a wee bit of pain."

Janey held him at arm's length. "What on earth have you done?" She noticed he was holding his arm carefully.

"It's nothing, honestly. I was putting the tent up and tripped over a guy. I came down on my arm; it's probably just a strain."

"And of course you won't have had it checked out I suppose."

"Don't come all nursey with me Mum, it's nothing." Fraser grinned at her and gave her a tentative hug and a kiss.

Janey looked at her watch. "There's a surgery on in the town, and If we're quick we could get you checked over. They'll see you as a visitor. I expect they're used to it with all the tourists."

"Please don't fuss, I don't want to spoil our day together."

"You'll spoil it a lot more if you don't let me help. I'll get your rucksack, come on, get in the car."

The drove into the town and parked outside the doctor's surgery. Janey helped Fraser out of the car and they went in.

"Hello, I'm hoping you can help my son." Janey addressed the smiling receptionist. "He's had a fall and done something to his arm. Is there any chance he could get it checked out? We live in Edinburgh and I'm working for the season at Aigas and Fraser is visiting me for the day."

"Let me have a word and we'll see what we can do. Just fill in this visitors' form."

"Do you need a help with that darling?"

"I think I can fill in a form, Mum, but thanks for this, it really is sore."

Janey kissed him on the cheek. "It doesn't matter how old you let get, you're always my wee lad."

Fraser smiled.

"The doctor will see you now, just go to the second door on the left." The receptionist pointed along the corridor.

Janey and Fraser went into the room, and were met by the doctor. All Janey noticed were the twinkling blue eyes and the warm smile. He looked older than Janey, but not by much she suspected. He shook her hand and it was like a shock through her arm at his touch. This was ridiculous. She pulled herself together.

"Hello, I'm Iain Raeburn, locum GP, how can I help?" He went to shake Fraser's hand then noticed he was cradling his left arm. "It's your arm then?"

"Yes." Fraser sat down as Iain indicated. "I was pitching a tent and tripped over a guy rope."

"Let's have a look then." Iain gently examined his arm. "I don't think you've broken anything. It just feels like bad bruising so I expect you'll be very sore for a while. So painkillers and rest should do the trick. I'll give you a sling, which should help. How long are you here for?"

"I'm just here for the day visiting mum then I'm back to Inverness this evening and Edinburgh on Tuesday."

"Edinburgh, that's where I work now, I'm just up here covering for a few weeks. How about Mum, where does she stay?" Iain smiled at Janey and she felt herself blushing. Did he have any idea what effect he was having on her?

"I live there too, I'm working at Aigas until Christmas, then heading back."

"Ah, with John, he does excellent work and it's a beautiful place. Well, I think your boy's going to live, he just need a bit of TLC."

"Thank you doctor, and thank you for fitting Fraser in, it's much appreciated."

"No problem, we often have to fit in a few extra patients, especially during the tourist season." He turned to Fraser, "If it's still sore when you get back Fraser, maybe pop into Chalmers for an X-ray. I'll give you a referral, it's a walk-in clinic, so if the arm's much better, no need to bother. Here, just in case you need it."

"Thanks doc, that's great."

Janey and Fraser got up to go. Iain extended his hand to Janey. She wondered if she was imagining it, but did he hold her hand just a fraction too long? "Thanks again Doctor." Janey didn't know what else to say.

"Iain is fine, no formalities."

"Janey," she stuttered. "Better be getting along."

They left the surgery and got back into the car. Janey pulled out of the car park.

"Well, Mum, maybe it's a good thing I hurt my arm."

"What are you talking about?"

"You don't fool me, Ma, I saw the looks between you and Dr Kildare. You're in there."

"Don't be silly; he was just doing his job. Just being friendly."

"Oh really? First name terms. Hope he's not your doctor. Oaths and all that."

"Actually, I'm signed up with the other practice, but they don't do a Saturday morning surgery, otherwise I'd have taken you there."

"Well, another lucky coincidence, Mum, let's hope you bump into him."

"Shut up Fraser," Janey chided him good naturedly, "I don't need a man."

"Oh yes you do, you deserve happiness and the doc was definitely interested. I know it."

"Change the subject. I'm meeting Katie. Do you want to join us?"

"I'll just leave you two to it I think, I'm not staying round for girly gossip. Maybe we could meet up later for a coffee before I get my train. I'm just going to go walkabout in Beauly."

"Will you be OK with your arm?"

"No need to worry, it feels a lot more comfortable in this sling. I'll pop a couple of paracetamols and I'll be fine. The lads will all help when I get back to Inverness. We're thinking about booking into the hostel anyway for the next couple of nights. The weather looks like it's going to turn bad tonight. I'll give them a call and sort that out."

"Well that would be one less thing for me to worry about." Janey pulled in beside the bookshop where she was meeting Katie for lunch. "Please take care, love. How about we meet back here about four o'clock?"

Fraser leaned over and kissed his mum on the cheek. "Thanks mum, that would be great. I'll take it easy and then you can drive me back to the station after you buy me an early dinner."

Janey laughed. "Of course. Get off with you and I'll see you later."

Fraser gave her a cheery wave with his good arm and strode off in the direction of the priory. That will keep him busy for a while, Janey thought to herself. He'll get lost in the history and he'll be happy as a sand boy. She watched Fraser as he walked away. My bonnie lad, she thought, I'm so lucky.

Janey went into the bookshop café, Katie was already there. "Hey, you're early, or did I get the time wrong?" she asked Katie as she sat down at the pretty window table.

"I just thought I'd catch up on some reading, Betty has some great books here." Katie put her book down. "I've just ordered a coffee; do you want one or will we just order an early lunch?"

"A coffee would be fine. I've had a tough morning so far." Janey sighed, sounding tired.

"What's happened, I thought you were meeting Fraser form the train?" "Oh, I did, and he'd hurt his arm so I took him to the surgery to get it checked. I got to check out the locum GP. Very nice."

"You didn't chat up the GP while your darling baby was poorly. Did you?"

"No, but there was a spark there. Haven't felt that for a while. I hope I bump into him again sometime."

"So, my friend, no-one on the horizon for ages and then two at once? Speaking of that, when are you having your meeting with David?"

"I do not have two turning up at once. Anyway, I said I'd meet David for supper at the pub this evening."

"Meeting him for supper, that's a turn up for the books, no pun intended, considering where we are." Katie looked round at the shelves stacked high with books.

"You could always meet him and stay over in the village if the weather turns bad," Katie suggested with a gleam in her eye.

"No way, I'm going to postpone our business meeting till next week, there's no drama. I'm on breakfast duty in the morning so I'd rather get back tonight after I drop Fraser at the station. The weather is closing in, so I'll go back to Aigas."

"Well, as long as it doesn't trouble us, I've been looking forward to a good natter." Katie sipped her coffee. "What do you think of him though, David I mean?"

"Stop fishing and eat your scone. I'm not interested in David. He's not my type." The doctor was though, thought Janey. Even though they'd only met briefly, he had her interest. No point in hoping, but fun to dream about.

"Are you biased because he's got ginger hair, that would be very politically incorrect?"

"Certainly not, I go for personality just as much as looks and for your information, if I was being completely objective, I'd say he was definitely very good looking in a roguish sort of way."

"You've had a good look then," Katie was smiling over her cup. "Maybe he'll grow on you."

"No way, he's too charming for me, I'd never be sure about him, he seems like a nice guy with too much of a fondness for the ladies."

"You shouldn't listen to gossip." Katie put her cup down. "Hugh says he's a good guy, just been unlucky in love. You should give him a chance. Get to know him, he's got a great sense of humour."

"God, what are you, a walking lonely hearts ad?" Janey laughed at her friend. "I'm happy being single at the moment, no time for a love interest. Too much to do and see. I don't need any ties, I've had nearly twenty-five years of those; I don't need any more."

"It's a long time since your divorce; live a little on the love front." Katie sounded quite earnest.

"I've not been living like a nun and well, you know, now the kids are nearly away I just want to think about me for a change."

Katie sighed, "I think he was quite smitten with you, you know, even Hugh said so."

"What, did you two have time to talk about me? You must be slacking, I thought you and Hugh were all about lust." Janey opened her eyes wide with feigned shock.

"I think it's more than plain old lust, although I'm not complaining."

Janey saw a shadow cross Katie's face. "What is it, a flaw in the big bold highlander? Cross words already?" Janey sounded flippant, but she was thinking back to her own suspicions about Hugh.

"Nothing really, no cross words or anything. But I really like him. I mean really, really, like him. And I'm almost sure he feels the same, but sometimes I think he's holding back on me about something." Janey's heart sank and she felt a shiver despite the warmth of the coffee shop. Katie continued, "I even asked him how he felt about a long-term relationship when he mentioned that he thought that's what David needed."

"Wow, that's a big deal. What did he say?"

"Well that's the thing, he seemed to answer without actually saying anything and then got off the subject."

"That would be the big kiss to throw you off the scent."

Katie frowned, "What do you mean "off the scent"?"

Janey felt bad about her off-the-cuff remark. "Nothing, nothing, just a turn of phrase, all I meant was that a nice big lusty kiss would stop most of us from asking any more questions." Janey could feel her face getting hotter, she was a bad liar at the best of times and Katie could generally read her like a book.

"And what other questions do you suppose I should have asked him?" Katie was on the defensive.

Janey sensed she was getting in far too deep with this topic and attempted to change the subject. "Are you meeting him tonight?"

Katie took the bait. "Yes, later, he's taking me out for a meal. Some out of the way restaurant that specialises in Scottish food. That's if the weather holds, I don't fancy driving there and back in the pouring rain or snow if this storm's as bad as the forecast. We might just settle for a fish supper and a wee cuddle. The room's got a cheery coal fire, very romantic."

"Sounds lovely." Janey inwardly sighed with relief, but felt very guilty. Maybe that would have been the moment to share her suspicions with Katie. Janey knew she was going to have to say something to Katie. Her heart fluttered and her stomach churned and not in a nice way. Janey would have to choose her words carefully. There wasn't going to be an easy way to say something, but Janey knew she couldn't keep quiet. If their situations were reversed Janey would want to know, and she was sure that even if they fell out, their long friendship would surely survive.

Katie paused as she took another sip of her coffee, cup mid-air. "I hope the storm doesn't stop Hugh from getting here later."

"What time are you meeting him?" Janey asked.

"He was working early today. Again. So we're meeting at three and going to Inverness? A bit of shopping for me and then dinner?"

Katie's face clouded over again. Janey held her breath as she wondered what Katie was thinking.

"Maybe if we stayed in Beauly tonight and the storm got really bad, he'd have to stay over." Katie spoke as though to herself. "He's never stayed the night Janey, never. He always has some excuse to sneak off."

"Oh, I'm sure he's hardly sneaking off. Maybe he's working early. That can mean four in the morning you know. The rangers all start early." Janey tried to sound reassuring. This was so hard, Janey knew she should say something but the wrong words kept coming out.

"But he must get some days off at the weekends, look at you. You manage it."

Janey was caught. "But I'm house staff, the rangers sometimes have to do more than their rota." Why was she defending this man that she was so suspicious of? Why didn't she just tell Katie that if you added a lot of the facts together, you could easily come up with someone who couldn't stay over because of a wife somewhere. A wife he was probably giving the 'working long hours' excuse to as well.

Katie pushed her cup away, the coffee forgotten. "What you said just now about the big kiss to throw me off the scent, you don't think he's hiding anything really big do you?"

Janey felt the flush on her face and knew Katie had noticed.

Katie's voice was a whisper and Janey knew that was bad news. Her friend always got quiet about things that really mattered; Katie shouting at her would have been far more comfortable.

"What are you hiding Janey? What do you know?"

Chapter 44

"Don't worry, I quite understand. The weather can be quite unpredictable this time of year." David hid the disappointment in his voice as he took the call on his mobile. "No problem, give me a call next week when I'm at work and we'll fit something in to the diary. I can see you in Inverness, but the office in Beauly would probably be better for you." David paused while Janey replied. "Wednesday should be fine. If you're shopping in Inverness, maybe we could catch some lunch?" He hoped he didn't sound too keen.

"Of course, I know your time's limited during the week with meals to prepare. I'll call you on Monday to confirm. Bye."

Damn, he'd been really looking forward to meeting Janey on her own. He'd been quite bowled over with her at the pub the evening before. She was quiet, but had a sharp wit. And very pretty. He guessed she'd be early forties, but when she'd talked about her kids, her realised she was older than she looked. When she'd shaken out her long dark hair from the hat she'd been wearing to keep out the cold, he could have done a lot more than kiss her hand. He thought he'd probably blown it with her and was anxious to make amends. He knew he had a bit of a reputation as an outrageous flirt, and had had a few dalliances while in Inverness, but only because nothing serious had come along. Until now. David didn't really believe in love at first sight, but this was something close. He hoped Janey was playing hard to get rather than hinting to him to get lost. She had seemed a bit distracted when she'd agreed to meet him for supper, but he hoped he'd get another chance. Damn this storm. Still, the course of true love had never run smoothly for him. He'd make sure he was just himself when they met, not the flirty Casanova he'd become to hide his true self. He knew he used the charm to cover up for all the hurt he'd felt when his marriage broke up. Maybe it was time he let his more sensitive side show, if he was ever going to find love again.

He'd loved his wife once, but her greed of money and utter selfishness had driven it out of him. He was well shot of his ex. Not that it stopped her calling him from time to time to moan about money. It was nothing to do with him now; he'd settled generously with her, even handed over the house. And what thanks did he get – more grief. As if it was all his fault that she now had a limited income. She didn't seem to understand they'd been divorced for years and it was up to her now. That she couldn't speak to him in the outrageous way she'd always done. Still, the last time she'd called he'd spelt it out to her in no uncertain terms that she was nothing to do with him now.

Every time he got the raging phone call, the verbal abuse for abandoning her then the tears, he swore he'd hang up the next time. He'd started trying that and it seemed to work. She hadn't called for a while now. Thank God she lived at the other end of the country. He was sure if he was still working in Ayr she'd be on his doorstep giving him grief.

He pushed all the bad thoughts from him and concentrated on the road. The storm was bad, so it was probably just as well Janey had cancelled. There was tree litter all over the road, and the puddles at the side of the road were threatening to flood. The rain was icy, and David knew that snow wasn't far away. The wind howled loudly; he could hear it even from the comfort of his car. He wouldn't have liked to think of Janey battling this in the estate's wee car on her way back to Aigas. He smiled to himself as he thought of her. She'd touched a soft spot, that was for sure. He was relieved she was already back there, even though it meant he had missed his chance to see her. Roll on Wednesday.

Chapter 45

Janey was glad to be back at Aigas. The storm and lashing rain looked far better from within the warmth of the big house. She wasn't worried about letting David down, it was just business after all, she assured herself. Maybe it wasn't such a bad thing; she'd maybe given him the wrong signal by agreeing to supper the evening after they'd only just met. He'd caught her on the hop when he'd asked; she was busy worrying about Hugh and had said yes to David before she'd really had a chance to think. He'd been sweet on the phone, quite understanding, but she thought he'd sounded just a little disappointed. Don't flatter yourself, missy, she thought, he's probably just as understanding to all his clients. Not that she was a client yet, she'd listen carefully to what he said before agreeing to anything. Getting enough to live on from her investment was the most important thing. Once she had that sorted, she could look around for something else to do after Christmas. John had made it clear she'd be welcome to work at Aigas again once the Easter season started. But Janey had been inspired during the conversation at the pub about the Edinburgh Book Festival. How good would it be to work in her own city during the festival, soaking up the entire atmosphere? She hadn't the faintest idea how to go about getting a job there, but she was sure there'd be some information on the website.

It was quiet in the house now, food served, the guests in the communal lounge enjoying a drink and reminiscing about the day past and chatting about the day to come. They'd all had to come back early, as she'd done, because of the storm, but they were enjoying the comfort the big house had to offer.

Janey was glad of the silence in the kitchen as she put the last of the dishes away. She needed some time to gather her thoughts and if she went back to her cabin, Lindsay would be there. She didn't feel like company just at the moment. Not until she had the tears properly under control. She'd been fine while she was busy with the others, preparing and serving the meal, but they were threatening to spill over again as she remembered the lunchtime disaster.

Janey had been very upset when she'd returned from Beauly earlier.

"Are you OK, Janey?" Lucy had asked gently.

"Oh, I'm fine, I'm just back from seeing Fraser onto the Edinburgh train. He's hurt his arm and we had to go to the local surgery. Luckily it's just bad bruising, but chatting to him over a quick meal was so lovely." Janey felt bad about lying to Lucy, she was so kind, but she could hardly tell her about the furious row she and Katie had had when Janey had finally confessed to Katie her suspicions, including the picture she'd seen of Hugh when she was in Majorca.

Katie had gone mad. Not in a loud, shouting kind of way -but in a quiet, scathing way.

"So he knocks you back for me, and you call that suspicious behaviour, you see some old photo of him in Majorca taken God knows when and meaning precisely nothing. You gossip with some foreign diving guy who probably wants into your pants and assume it's suspicious because he lives in a remote bothy instead of at Aigas with your silly gossipy workmates. You try to find out anything about him by asking sneaky questions behind his back and assume that because he can't spend the night with me he's got a wife squirreled away somewhere. How low can you get, Janey?" Janey had tried to interject, to explain it again how she saw things but Katie was having none of it. She wouldn't let Janey say another word.

"I don't know why you have these suspicions Janey, it's not like you to accuse before you know all the facts. Are you still holding a candle for Hugh? He's with me now, get used to it."

"That's ridiculous…" Janey knew Katie would mistake the colour in her cheeks for guilt rather than frustration that Katie wouldn't look at circumstances from Janey's point of view.

Katie broke into her reply, "I can see it in your face. What were you going to do, Janey, offer him a soft shoulder to cry on once I'd flounced back to Edinburgh? Well stuff you. I'd know if he was married; he'd have told me. And if there's an ex somewhere in the dim distant past, that's our business. For all you know he's explained all of that and we don't want the whole world to know. Especially when there's busybodies like you, poking their noses where they're definitely not wanted and making fantastical stories out of utter nonsense. I don't need a friend like you, Janey. Just leave us alone."

Even though Katie had almost hissed at her during the outburst, one or two of the other customers had looked up from their coffees, sensing an atmosphere. Janey had tried to protest but Katie had stood up and stormed out of the shop.

By the time Janey had settled the bill with Betty who looked at her questioningly and hurried out to the street, Katie was nowhere to be seen. The storm was getting worse, no worse than the storm between her and Katie, Janey thought. The wind was biting and it had started to rain heavily. She knew she should get back to Aigas while she could. Janey thought about ringing the bell at the bed and breakfast where Katie was staying, but thought the better of it. Katie just needed time to calm down. Maybe she'd realise why Janey had been suspicious. But then maybe not. She was clearly defending the man she was falling in love with and she knew Katie well enough to know whose side she'd be on.

It had all gone horribly wrong. Janey wished she'd said something earlier. Listening to Katie had made her feel terrible. When Katie put the facts as she had, it was no wonder she'd thought Janey was jealous. But she really wasn't. She'd long got over the fact that Hugh wasn't interested in her, and seeing Katie and him together only made Janey feel glad that he'd chosen to continue to see Katie. The day was getting worse and worse, the weather reflecting Janey's mood. She felt hot tears on her cheeks and turned towards the car. It was too much to hope that Katie wouldn't mention her suspicions to Hugh. So she'd probably get an earful from him. She felt like packing her bags and heading right back to Edinburgh to lick her wounds. But that was the coward's way out. She'd have to face the music and put up with the consequences. She just hoped it wouldn't cause an atmosphere at work. Not when she was getting on so well. She got in the car, unsure what to do.

She'd take a detour to the Moniac Winery before meeting Fraser and get herself a couple of bottles of wine. She had a couple of hours yet so she could kill some time wandering around the winery. She knew she'd burst into tears if anyone spoke to her, and she didn't fancy having to explain herself or make any excuses. The winery was quiet, so she took the tour with a few tourists and it allowed her to regain her composure. She was busy concentrating on which wine to buy when she became aware of someone coming to stand behind her. She turned and looked up into those gorgeous blue eyes that had set her heart racing just a few hours ago.

"Hello Janey, anything you fancy here?"

Janey didn't give the answer that sprung to her lips. *You.* "Just having a look, if the storm gets worse there'll be no clubbing for me tonight, just a good book and a fine bottle of wine."

"Didn't have you down for the clubbing type." Iain smiled at her and she smiled warmly back.

"Well of course I am, always out clubbing in Edinburgh." They both laughed. Janey felt strangely relaxed in his company, which was odd as she hardly knew this man.

"Yes, me too. But I'd rather share a meal and wine in the comfort of a good restaurant."

"Me too, I'm afraid my clubbing days are over, if they ever started."

"So, what wine do you like? I love the selection here and it's good to support local business." Iain reached past her and picked up a bottle of red. "They say a glass or two of this is good for you."

Janey felt the closeness of him as he reached across for the wine. It was a good feeling.

"I enjoy the wines I like, I drink anything. Sorry, that makes me sound like an alcoholic. I mean the colour isn't as important as the taste." Janey knew she was wittering, but couldn't seem to help herself. Stupidly, she could feel the tears welling up again.

"I'm much the same. Hey, what's wrong? Not something I said?" Ian put his hand gently on her shoulder. The tears fell.

"I'm so sorry, I don't know what's got into me. I fell out with a friend earlier and I'm feeling bad about it. Ignore me."

"I don't think anyone could ignore you Janey. Come on let's go for a coffee and you can tell me all about it. You can trust me, I'm a doctor."

The absurd over-used statement brought a smile to her face.

"That's my line." she smiled wanly, "Trust me, I'm a nurse."

"A nurse, and I thought you were one of John's rangers." Iain guided her gently to the coffee shop in the winery. They sat down and Iain ordered two coffees, allowing Janey to gain her composure.

The coffee duly arrived. "Thank you Iain, sorry about that, I'm OK now. I used to be a nurse and then lately I've been working in a supermarket, it's convenient to work around the family. And now I'm working in the house at Aigas, I'm far too old to be a ranger."

Iain smiled at her and she caught her breath. "So what brought you here, or are you like me and just need a highland tonic once in a while?"

"I got the chance to make some changes in my life and now that Fraser is settled at university, I thought it was my time to something for myself. I'm just here until Christmas then it's back to Edinburgh to decide what to do next."

"That sounds fascinating. I do a locum her every year, but my practice is in Edinburgh. I always feel that working up here feels like a holiday."

"That's exactly what I was saying to friends last night." Janey smiled at him, wondering how she'd managed to fall so easily into conversation with this stranger.

"Then that's something we have in common then."

The conversation flowed easily after that, and the next hour found Janey telling Iain all sorts of things, and he was just as chatty as her.

"Oh, I really have to go. I'm meeting Fraser for a catch up before he goes back to Inverness. He sent me a text to say he and his mates have booked into a hostel for the next two nights, so the tents are packed up. I'm glad, it will be more comfortable with his arm the way it is. He said he was feeling better with the sling."

"Glad to hear it, but I'm sorry you have to go. Fancy continuing our conversation over dinner sometime? Here's my card, just give me a call."

Janey scribbled her mobile number on a page torn from her diary. "Here's mine. It's been lovely chatting, I'm sorry I have to go."

"Come on then, I'll get the coffee and buy you a bottle of wine, so you can think of me while you drink it." Ian grinned at Janey and planted a kiss on her cheek.

She smiled back. "Thank you Iain, and thanks for listening, I feel much better now." They headed for the exit, Iain carrying a couple of bottles.

"Enjoy the wine Janey, next time I'll throw in a meal."

"Speak soon then." Janey floated out of the winery clutching her wine. She got into her car and waved back at Iain as she drove away. Minutes later she was sitting with Fraser enjoying his chat, laughing with him and forgetting her troubles with Katie for a while. She dropped him at the station and waved him away with the usual mum comments about taking care and making him promise to let her know how his arm was. A hug and a kiss and her big laddie was gone.

She started towards the Aigas road. Maybe some of that magic would work for her now. As she drove, avoiding the bits of trees already falling on to the road, she remembered David. She'd have to call him as soon as she got back. Even without the storm, she couldn't have faced him. Janey didn't think she'd feel much like socialising after dinner that evening, so she'd curl up in her cabin with a good book and a glass or two of wine.

Janey was glad to see the welcoming lights of Aigas greet her as it came in to view from the sweeping bend. She'd be content for the evening and maybe Katie would speak to her the next day.

She drove up the long drive and looked with dismay as she saw Hugh on the big stone steps. He didn't look like the welcoming party. Clearly he'd already spoken to Katie. Damn. She parked and turned towards her cabin, pretending she hadn't seen him, or had no reason to speak to him. Three strides and he'd caught up with her.

"A word if you don't mind." Hugh caught her by the arm and marched her into the shelter of the car-port. "Just what the hell do you think you're playing at?"

Chapter 46

Katie was furious. How could she? she thought, as she stormed out of the bookshop coffee shop. It's the happiest I've been for a very long time and she just wants to spoil it. Katie knew in her heart that Janey wasn't after Hugh, but the bitter words had spilt out. She'd show her, prove to her that Hugh had nothing to hide. That he was just a private man, unused to sharing all his thoughts. Katie paid no heed to the heavy rain and fierce wind. She couldn't go back to the bed and breakfast, she couldn't face the kindly owners. She'd intended to spend the early afternoon cosily chatting with Janey but that was in ruins now. She crossed the square and went in to the nearest shop, the hairdresser. She didn't want to see Janey and knew she'd never think to follow her here. She stood dripping inside the shop door, uncertain what to do next.

"Can I help you dear?" The middle-aged woman approached her.

"I'm not sure." Katie was trembling with rage.

"Do you have an appointment?"

"Em, no."

"We can probably fit you in, we're not too busy, what would you like?"

The woman picked a coat hanger from the stand beside the door and held out her hand for Katie's dripping coat.

The shop was warm and the woman friendly. Katie felt close to tears. She knew she looked a sight, windswept and soaked. "It's a fierce storm brewing, come away and sit down. Would you like a cup of tea?"

The woman's concern made the tears spill over. Katie felt such a fool, the other workers in the shop giving her sidelong glances and the customers trying to see what was going on at the door without turning their heads.

"I'm fine, really." Katie's voice wobbled as she tried to sound normal.

"Of course, it's just the storm," the kindly woman showed her to a seat in the waiting area and hung up Katie's coat, "have a seat while you decide."

Katie sank thankfully onto the seat and the woman sat beside her.

"My name's Sue. You just take your time and I'll get you tea. What do you take?"

"Just black thanks. I take all my drinks neat." Katie managed a feeble smile and Sue was kind enough to laugh at her little joke.

"A woman after my own heart. I'll just be back."

Katie sat back and tried to calm herself. There were worse places to be, and maybe a bit of pampering was in order after her row with Janey. She picked up a magazine and pretended to read it.

Sue came back with her tea and Katie felt a bit better.

"Just a trim would be fine, thanks."

"No problem, nothing like having your hair done to make you feel better. Do you want it washed and dried as well?"

"Yes please." The hot tea was a good antidote to her wounded feelings.

"Pop over here then. Jackie, would you wash…"

"Katie, Katie Brown."

"….Mrs Brown's hair please?"

"Katie would be fine; Mrs Brown makes me feel old."

"Well then, Katie, you get your hair washed and we'll decide what to do."

Sue smiled warmly at her. Hairdressers had a habit of putting folk at their ease, Katie thought. Katie had had the same hairdresser for a long time back in Edinburgh. In fact no one else had ever cut her hair since she was in her teens. In for a penny, she took a deep breath and leaned her head back for Jackie to wash.

"Conditioner?" Jackie asked as Katie felt the warm water not only wetting her hair but soothing her too.

"Yes please, but only one shampoo."

"Right-o then." Jackie began to massage in the shampoo.

Katie realised she hadn't even checked out the price, but surely it wouldn't be high street prices here. Anyway, she didn't care. She was already feeling much better, and having her hair done would not only kill some time but she'd feel better meeting Hugh with newly styled hair. What was she going to say to him? She could hardly ignore what Katie had said, she'd have to say something to him. She was sure he'd clear up any nagging doubts. Nagging doubts, Katie thought with a start, surely Janey's suspicions hadn't rubbed off on her. She trusted Hugh and he'd never given her any reason to think he was married. Except perhaps the rushing off in the early hours and his refusal to spend a whole night with her? Katie pushed the thought aside. She'd speak to him calmly and see what he said. Jackie wrapped the towel around her head and showed her to one of the chairs in front of the mirror. As she was waiting for Sue, her mobile rang. It was Hugh. Panic lurched inside her.

"Hi, you." Katie tried to sound cheery.

"Hi, where are you?" Her heart melted as she heard his lilting voice.

"I'm at the hairdressers getting all glammed up to see you." Hugh laughed.

"In this weather, the wind will sort that out and no problem."

"Not at all, at least you'll know I made the effort."

"You don't need to make an effort for me; you'd be gorgeous however you looked."

Katie felt the familiar tingle and smiled at his comment. "Flatterer, what are you wanting?"

"Just wait and see. How long will you be? In this weather it would be foolish to go to Inverness for a meal, I thought I'd meet you early, have a late lunch instead, in case the weather sets in."

"That fine, I should be finished in about half an hour."

She glanced questioningly at Sue who was waiting for her to finish before beginning her trim. Sue nodded.

"Half an hour then, at the Lovat Arms?"

"Perfect, see you then." Hugh hung up.

"Sorry, Sue, I'm keeping you back." Katie switched off her mobile.

"Och, that's just fine, boyfriends take precedence over me every day." Sue stood behind Katie and spoke to her in the mirror. "What are we having then?"

"Just a tidy up really, nothing drastic. I just had the colour done last week."

"And a bonny colour it is too. Are you visiting?"

"Yes, I've been a few times now, I live in Edinburgh but my boyfriend works here so I come up when I can."

"I trained in Edinburgh, got my City and Guilds at Telford College, a few years ago now though." Sue smiled at the memory. "I worked in the City for a while, but love brought me back here."

"The lengths we go to for our men." Katie warmed to Sue's calm chattiness.

They talked as Sue cut and Katie was aware that she was a very good hairdresser indeed. Even before Sue blew her hair dry, Katie was pleased with the cut.

"Have you worked here for long?" Katie asked her.

"Oh I own the place, bought it over when the last owner retired. Now, straight or that trendy tousled look?"

"Straight to start, I dare say the wind will give me the tousled look whenever I want it."

The two women laughed.

After Katie had paid (and very reasonable it was too) she held her coat over her head and crossed over the main road to the Lovat Arms. She prayed Janey hadn't hung about. Katie was feeling much calmer but had no desire to see Janey any time soon.

Hugh was waiting for her as she stepped into the warm pub from the gale outside. She took the coat from her head and shook her newly glossy locks. She was more than conscious that her make-up was all rubbed off. Between the tears and the hair washing, her face was clean as a whistle. She frowned, she should have done a quick repair at the hairdresser.

"Hey, what's this – greeting me with a frown?" Hugh stood up as she walked over and held her at arm's length.

"Oh, the rain washed my make-up off, I should have put more on across the road." Katie gazed up at him and melted.

"On a day like this, you needn't bother, you look lovely."

"Soppy thing." Katie smiled lovingly at him.

"No, romantic. And why not for the woman in my life?"

A shadow crossed Katie's face as she had the sudden unwelcome thought, am I the only woman in your life? She shrugged the thought away.

"I've got you a white wine, hope that's OK?"

Katie sat on the couch next to the roaring log fire and Hugh sat beside her, taking her hand. "Yes that's fine, although I probably need a triple whisky after the day I've had." Katie had muttered the last part of her reply, but Hugh picked her up on it.

"I thought you'd had a good day seeing Janey and catching up on all the gossip. In fact I was surprised when I called you and you were getting you hair done. I was sure I'd have to prise you away from Janey to get you to myself."

"Oh, she had to leave, had to get back…something…" Katie faltered and burst into tears.

"OK, what's happened, surely nothing to do with Janey, you two are such good friends."

"Yes. She said something I didn't like." Katie felt her heart thudding. She looked down at her hands, cupping Hugh's large hand between hers. She didn't want to spoil her time with Hugh but knew she'd be unable to keep up any sort of pretence with him.

"So tell me, what's the problem, I don't like to see you troubled, Katie, tell me."

His voice was so soft and warm, Katie could feel the tears threatening again. "We- we- fell out."

"Even I can tell that, what about?"

Katie took a deep breath and looked at Hugh. "About you." She said as steadily as she could.

"Me, why on earth would you fall out about me?" Hugh leaned towards her. "I hardly speak to Janey, no more or less than the other house staff, what am I supposed to have done?"

"Nothing, it's Janey and her wild ideas, I told her it was rubbish and that she was just meddling, but she was saying stupid things, so I told her what I thought, that I didn't believe any of it and left her in the coffee shop. I didn't know where to go and ended up in the hairdresser, so hid there for a bit. They were really nice and I needed a bit of a trim, so I went for it and now I feel much better. I'm so glad I'm here with you, you'll make it all better."

The words had spilled out with a rush and Katie hugged Hugh close to her.

"Whoa." Hugh disentangled himself and held Katie's hands. "What things, what did she say?" Hugh tried hard to control his expression, the sinking feeling in his stomach threatening to give him away.

"All sorts of stupid things." Katie took a deep breath. There was clearly no point in trying to convince Hugh that their fall out was about nothing. She might as well tell him and get it over with. "She seems to think you're hiding something."

Hugh paled. Katie was still studying her hands, and didn't notice. "What sort of something?" He held his breath.

"She thinks you're married and haven't told me." Katie couldn't bear to look at him, realising she was scared of his reply.

Hugh let out his breath. "Married." He said, his voice dull.

Katie felt as though her world was about to fall apart. Why didn't he say something? Reassure her it was all lies. She waited, resisting the urge to cut and run.

"No, Katie, I'm not married." His voice was low, but Katie sensed a relief in his tone. She hoped it was real. "Not any more."

Katie looked up at him, the question hanging between them reflected in his eyes.

"It was such a long time ago. In a former life. I know I should have told you, but I find it hard to find the words. It's all in the past. I was young; she was young. Family pressures made it all go wrong. And no kids."

Katie didn't want to ask if he meant "no kids" meant they'd wanted them or whether he meant there just hadn't been any. She was too scared to ask.

"Why didn't you say something? You know everything about me." Katie didn't want to sound petulant, but he didn't seem to notice.

"Sorry, Katie, it's just something I can't talk about. Let's leave it for now. I'll tell you all about it soon. I promise I will, and when I do everything will make sense." He sounded so dismissive she couldn't bring herself to say more.

"OK, let's not spoil the evening; we can talk about it all some other time." Katie sat upright.

She wasn't sure how she felt. There seemed to be a distance between them, a new feeling. One she didn't like, but thought she'd said enough. She glanced at Hugh and noted the tightness in his jaw and what she thought was anger in his eyes.

"Tell you what." Hugh pulled himself up and turned to Katie. "You're right, let's not waste the evening. I know the storm is bad, so let's forget about Inverness and dinner; but let me pop home, tidy up and I'll come back into Beauly. You go back to the bed and breakfast, have a good long soak and I'll call in for you in an hour, then we can start the evening again. What do you think?"

Before she could answer, he kissed her tenderly. She felt the passion rising and knew she was powerless to resist. Whatever her misgivings, she'd trust him. Even though there was a nagging doubt growing. She wanted to ask if he'd stay the night. But she didn't want to hear the answer. She prayed Janey was wrong.

Chapter 47

Hugh hurried to his Land Rover after seeing Katie back to the bed and breakfast.

Bloody woman, he thought. *Bloody, bloody interfering woman.* He hated lying to Katie, but he'd missed his chance to explain. He'd wanted to speak to her in his own time, not because some stupid, nosey, city girl who fancied herself as an amateur sleuth dictated the time and place. He had to sort things at home and hopefully when he did get round to explaining to Katie she'd forgive him and try to understand. Meanwhile he had Janey to contend with. Hugh wasn't an angry man by nature, but she'd need to be told in no uncertain terms to back off. Hugh hated the thought that someone was trying to interfere in his private life.

He seethed all the way back to Aigas. He hoped Janey would be by herself in her cabin, he didn't fancy Lindsay as an audience, but he needed to let Janey know he wouldn't tolerate her interference any more. Hugh knew Janey had had a soft spot for him when they'd first met, but it shocked him to think she was prying into his private affairs. She didn't know the truth; she was just jumping to unfounded conclusions. After all, thought Hugh grimly, if he'd been seeing Janey it wouldn't have changed things for him now. Only what had changed was that he'd fallen in love with Katie at the wrong time. He hoped and prayed he could sort this mess out without hurting too many people.

He drove carefully up the drive to the house, the Aigas deer could be close by in this weather. He was surprised to see that Janey's car wasn't back in the car port. She must have gone somewhere else after leaving Katie.

Hugh parked and went into the house. He exchanged a few words with those in the kitchen then hovered in the entrance porch waiting for Janey to return.

She wasn't far behind him. Her car drove towards the house then she turned to park.

Hugh was sure she'd spotted him. Janey got out of the car and turned towards her cabin a little too quickly.

Hugh leapt down the steps and strode towards her and shouted to her, "A word if you don't mind." Hugh caught her by the arm and marched her into the shelter of the car-port. "Just what the hell do you think you're playing at?"

"Sorry, what…"

"You will be sorry. Very sorry." Hugh cut across her blustering, refusing to let Janey speak. "How dare you fill Katie's head with jealous crap? Who do you think you are?"

Hugh's tone was so ominous, Janey didn't dare reply. His hand was biting into her arm and she felt very afraid.

"What goes on between Katie and me is none of your business. And what goes on in my life is nothing, absolutely nothing to do with you. What we choose to talk about, or for that matter, not talk about is none of your fucking business, understand."

Janey nodded.

"Do you understand?" Hugh dropped her arm. He towered over her demanding a reply.

"Yes." Janey squeaked.

She didn't know what to do. She'd never seen the usually quiet, easy-going Hugh in such a fearsome temper.

"So stay out of my way – and out of Katie's way if you know what's good for you. Don't interfere in what you don't understand. Leave us alone." He turned and stormed back to the big house.

Janey stood for a moment rooted to the spot. Her mind was all over the place. This wasn't a Hugh she knew. She was pretty sure Katie would be surprised too, but that was hardly a concern at the moment. She was sure she'd been threatened but why? What did he have to hide that would make him so angry?

Janey crept out of the car-port and hurried to her cabin. She needed time to think. She made herself a coffee and sat in front of the fire. Lindsay was out so she wouldn't have to explain the trembling in her hands. She went back to the little kitchen and poured herself a glass of the wine she'd bought. She needed a drink to steady her nerves. Now she was certain Hugh had something to hide. Not just from her, but from Katie as well. She needed a plan. Katie might have fallen out with her, but was sure that would change when the truth about Hugh came out. She'd risked her friendship with Katie already, now she had to find out exactly what Hugh was hiding, or rather who Hugh was keeping a secret. Janey was pretty sure now exactly what was going on.

She stepped out onto the balcony with her glass of wine and took a couple of deep breaths. She heard the Land Rover fire up, and then watched the headlights make a sweep in front of the house as Hugh drove off.

Back to see Katie for a cosy night now that he thinks he's shut me up, she thought. But I'll bet he doesn't stay over. I've got the measure of you, Hugh, I'm used to bullies, but you're not getting added to the list of ones I've had to put up with.

Janey put her wine glass in the kitchen. Lindsay would be back any minute and Janey didn't want to face her. She'd go over to the house and help tidy up after the meal. It would be finished by now and it would take her mind off things. She needed to be busy to try to quell the storm going on in her head as well as outside.

Chapter 48

Breakfast was over, the packed lunches made up and given out to the eager visitors and Janey relaxed with a cup of tea in front of the warm Aga in the kitchen of the big house. Lucy came over to join her.

"That's a good group we've got in this week, I'm glad the weather has cleared up today for them, they'll enjoy the trek."

Janey nodded. "You'd never think we had such a storm yesterday – apart from all the leaves and twigs blown all over the ground. The wind has dropped and the sun is glorious. It makes a pretty picture of all the autumn colours."

"That's what's so exciting about living here, hardly two days alike." Lucy nursed her cup. "Mind you, there's a nip in the air so it's likely winter's not far off. Are you going in to Beauly to see Katie today? I can start dinner myself if you want the afternoon off." Janey tried to sound up beat but she was sorry not to have at least talked to Katie before she went south. Still, maybe if she could get some concrete evidence about Hugh, Katie would see that she meant well and only had her friend's welfare at heart. "You're very pre-occupied today, is everything alright?" Lucy had that knack of thought reading sometimes and she was usually right.

"No, I'm fine, the wind kept waking me up last night, I'm just tired. If it's OK with you, Lucy, I'll give you a hand preparing for dinner, maybe take a stroll or even go into Beauly as it's my evening off if that's allowed?"

"No problem." Lucy laughed, "It's fine by me, we all need a bit or time off. It's not long till the end of the season now, then Christmas. Although I'm not sure which is busier, the guests visiting Aigas or the family descending for the season."

"I know what you mean, they're all coming to me this year and I love it, but it's almost too quiet when they all go back to their homes."

Janey smiled at Lucy, she had a wonderful calming effect and never seemed to get ruffled by anything.

They started the dinner preparations, Lucy never guessing that Janey was hatching her plan for later that night.

Chapter 49

Katie dozed as the steady rhythm of the train swept her south through the highlands. Hugh had come back to see her and they'd enjoyed a good meal then gone straight back to her room in the bed and breakfast. Katie almost thought of it as her room, the landlady made sure she always got the same one with its view over the main square in Beauly. Not that she and Hugh had been bothered about the view out of the window the previous night. They'd been too busy drinking in the view of each other. He'd been so passionate, most demanding in a quite delightful way, Katie could feel the warm ache he'd left after a night of lovemaking.

Well not quite a whole night. She'd been so deeply aroused and satisfied; she'd fallen in to a deep sleep and didn't even fully waken when she felt him slip out of the bed and away from her. She woke to the smell of bacon telling her it was breakfast time. She'd rolled over in bed and stretched out to him only to remember he'd left. Again. And he'd been so busy loving her, she hadn't asked him to stay. That night she was sure he would, they'd seemed so entwined in passion she couldn't understand what could possibly tear him away.

Unless Janey was right.

The thought jolted her upright, like a slap in the face. Janey couldn't be right. There was no way Hugh could be so loving if he had a wife stashed away.

Katie gave herself a reality check. Katie knew he could. Any man could, god knows she and her friends had had or heard of enough of them. There was the author she'd gone to see at the Edinburgh Book Festival who'd written a book about her bigamous husband who'd also been a convicted paedophile. But that was extreme. Surely her Hugh wasn't cheating on her.

She put the thoughts back in their box along with the guilt she felt about falling out with Janey and took out a book. No point in thinking the worst until it happens. As her mother used to say, "What will be, will be." Janey was one of Katie's oldest friends. She hated falling out with her. In fact they hadn't ever fallen out before that Katie could remember. Katie loved her like a sister and they had been through so much together. Maybe a bit if distance would let them both calm down a bit.

Katie just couldn't understand how Janey could jump to such a conclusion. Of course, Katie hadn't exactly let her explain fully. Maybe she just didn't want to hear anything that could possibly cast doubts about her relationship with Hugh. Well, things would work themselves out one way or another. Once she was feeling calmer, maybe they could talk about it.

Chapter 50

The skies were heavy with threatening rain, a contrast to the start of the day. In these parts, and at this time of year, it wasn't unusual to have all four seasons in one day. Janey looked out over the glen from the kitchen window as she prepared the evening meal.

Peeling the veg for the soup wasn't so bad she thought when you can look out at such a lovely view.

In all the time she'd been working at Aigas she'd not seen the same view twice from this window. She wondered if rain was on the way or if it was a heavy snow cloud coming their way.

Lucy broke into her thoughts as if she had read them.

"Snow coming, I think. This broth will be just perfect tonight." Lucy strained the beef stock into the big heavy soup pan.

"Do you think it will be heavy snow?" Janey took the peeled and chopped vegetables over to Lucy.

"Shouldn't be too bad," she replied, "But it's hard to tell. In all the years I've lived here, I still can't read the clouds like John can. He'll know. Are you OK Janey, you seem a bit distracted?"

"I'm fine," Janey replied, "I just had a bit of a run in with Katie and I'm going to have to sort it out. I'm not sure how though, she won't return my calls. She can be very stubborn."

"Maybe that's why you're such good friends," Lucy laughed, "You're very similar."

"I'm not that stubborn." Janey protested, "She can sulk for days you know."

"There's nothing worse than sulking, that's for sure. Maybe you're not stubborn. But you're determined when you set your mind to it. I was thinking of the time when you first came and couldn't get the log burner in the big hall to light. You wouldn't let anyone help and it took you an hour and a lot of curses to light it."

"That's perseverance. I wasn't going to let a log burner get the better of me. It became a battle of wills, but at least I got it lit in the end."

"You certainly did; and kept us all entertained in the process. I think everyone in the place was fascinated by the time you managed to light it."

"I know, I remember the round of applause." Janey smiled at the memory. "It's been lovely working here; I can't believe I only have so little time left."

"We'll miss you when you go, but there's always next season. You'd be welcome to come back in the spring. John and I have been talking and we'd be very happy if you'd come back."

"I'm not sure – not that I wouldn't love to – but I do miss Edinburgh. Of course by the time I get Christmas over, maybe I'll be pining for the highlands again. When would I have to let you know?"

"Oh, not until the beginning of the year, you take your time and let us know when you're ready."

"Thanks Lucy," Janey gave the older woman a hug, "You really are a good friend."

"And you've been a friend to me too. It's good to chat to another woman who understands about children and life."

"I'll certainly be taking some of your recipes back with me. We'll eat well this Christmas, lots of home cooking. This broth smells lovely."

"It's good to make it in the morning, then it can soak all day and be even tastier by the time six o'clock comes. Are you doing anything this afternoon Janey?"

"Depending on the weather, I think I'll go for a walk. Work up an appetite and take some photos for my Aigas album."

"I didn't know you were a photographer." Lucy dried her hands and moved over to turn the kettle on for their cup of tea.

"I'm not a photographer really but I've been taking a lot of pictures while I've been here. There seems to be a different aspect to the glen every day and I've even managed to get a few of the wildlife. And the scenery. And of course last month the fungi were spectacular. Nothing fancy, but a reminder of Aigas."

Lucy handed Janey her cup and sat down beside the Aga. "That's one of the things I love about Aigas. In the city you don't notice the weather or the different light nearly so much. Up here it means something, we run our lives by the weather and the seasons. If you're going any distance check with John or Hugh about the weather, and let them know the route you'll be taking. Just in case."

At the mention of Hugh, Janey paused as she lifted her cup to her lips. She wouldn't be able to tell anyone where she was planning to go. She knew Hugh was working in the afternoon, but as it was Sunday she also knew he'd leave Aigas and go home around four o'clock. She was going to follow him. She'd thought it all through. Janey was determined to find out once and for all exactly what Hugh was up to. If she was wrong about him and he simply lived on his own, she could apologise to Katie and enjoy the fact her friend had found happiness. On the other hand, if he had a wife stashed away somewhere she would... well she wasn't exactly sure what she'd do, but she'd do something. Maybe Lucy was right – maybe she was stubborn. She sipped her tea and dragged her thoughts back to Lucy and the kitchen.

"I'll do that. If I do go into Beauly, don't worry if I'm not here for dinner. I'll get something there."

Janey added the last thought so that no one would think it odd if she went out and wasn't back when it got dark.

"No problem, we'll see you later, have fun." Lucy finished drying her cup. "I'm off upstairs, there's a book with my name on it and I intend to give myself a couple of hours before I put the roast in for dinner." Lucy left the kitchen to go to her cosy private apartment.

Janey left the house by the kitchen door and headed for her cabin. Lindsay was away for the weekend and wouldn't be back until Monday so Janey had the place to herself. She'd go for a short walk, fix herself some lunch and follow Lucy's plan and curl up with a book until it was time for a bit of detective work. She'd be ready to follow Hugh later and try to solve the mystery she was so sure about. She felt very nervous at the thought of it. If Hugh caught her, she wasn't sure what he'd do. She'd already seen first-hand how angry he could get, and she didn't fancy her chances if he should find her out. But it was worth it to sort out her friendship with Katie. Sometimes you just have to take a risk and see what happens.

With that thought, Janey walked up to the small loch behind the house keeping a wary eye on the heavy clouds gathering threateningly above.

Chapter 51

The first flakes of snow were falling as Janey got back to the cabin. Maybe her plan was a bit mad with the weather closing in, but the sooner she found out the truth, the sooner she could mend the rift between her and Katie. She unlaced her walking boots and shrugged off her fleece. She'd lit the fire before she'd gone on her walk, so tossing on another log she fixed herself something to eat. Sitting in the old armchair beside the cosy fire, the thought of following Hugh on what promised to be a wintry evening seemed quite daunting. Still, it had to be done. She picked up her book, determined to switch off from her troubles for a couple of hours. *44 Scotland Street* beckoned. She was half way through the book and looking forward to losing herself in the story again. The heat of the open fire took its toll and she could feel herself dosing. I'll just close my eyes for a few minutes, she thought, sleepily closing the book and relaxing into the comfort of the big armchair.

When she woke with a start it was dark outside and the fire had died right down. Damn, she cursed out loud, what on earth was the time? She turned on the lamp and looked at her watch. Half past three. She'd slept for two hours, but not too late to put her plan into action. She donned her fleece and her cagoule, stuffing a pair of gloves into her pocket along with her mobile phone which she'd charged earlier. An extra pair of socks under my walking boots should keep my feet warm, she thought, pulling them on. She shoved a couple of chocolate bars into her pockets as well. Just in case. As she readied herself to go out, Janey had a thought. There was an obvious flaw in her plan. Hugh would recognise any vehicle following him. Even if she only tried to follow him to any turn off he should take, she had no idea of where he lived or how far it might be from the main road. She nearly called the whole mad escapade off, but then had a brainwave. Why hadn't she thought of it before? It was genius. She put the fireguard on after stoking up the fire, closed the curtains and left the cabin. She walked quickly down the path, past the railway lamp and over to the covered car port.

Thank goodness, his Land Rover was still there. As quickly as she could, she clambered into the back and under the tarpaulin. Something vaguely unpleasant assaulted her nose. There had been something decidedly smelly in the back before her. She lay very still; glad she'd wrapped up well and waited. Snow was falling, not too heavy yet, but she hoped she wouldn't have to wait for too long before Hugh decided to go home. She should have brought a torch. Janey didn't dare risk going to get one now. With her luck Hugh would catch her climbing out, or even back in, and she'd no idea what she'd say in her defence. She had a sudden panic. What if he's got something to take home that he'd going to dump in the back where she was? In changing from her first plan, she'd clearly not thought this one through at all. Maybe she should sneak out and just stay put in the cabin. She was on the verge of doing just that when she heard feet crunching across the driveway. Too late, Janey, she chided herself, you'll just have to go with the flow now.

She heard Hugh whistling some tune she only vaguely recognised and felt the Land Rover rock as he climbed into the driver's seat. He closed the door and Janey could no longer hear him from her hiding place. She felt the engine spark into life, then he drove off. It was a bumpy ride in the back but the loudest thing she could hear was her own heart. She must be stark raving bonkers to be doing this. What on earth was had she been thinking of?

Janey was gripped by the most appalling thought as she felt the Land Rover pull onto the main road and speed up. She was so stupid. It suddenly dawned on her that she had absolutely no idea where she was going. At least if she'd managed to follow him discretely in the car she'd have a vague idea of where he lived, but she was as blind as a new born puppy on this adventure. And she couldn't even be sure he was going home. Maybe he had another mistress he visited on Sunday evenings once Katie had gone home. Her overactive imagination was playing at maximum overdrive now. *Idiot, Idiot, Idiot. Maybe if he slows down I could jump out and walk home.* Then the next appalling thought raced into her mind. *Even if he goes straight home, what do I do then? I might be able to see who's there, but if I do, how do I get back?* Janey closed her eyes tight. Maybe she was just having a vivid dream and would waken beside the cosy fire. She opened her eyes. No, this wasn't a dream, it was still pitch black under the tarpaulin and the Land Rover was still driving along at quite a pace. And even if she did jump out she'd have no idea where she was. She peeked out of the side, guessing Hugh's driving blind spot to avoid being noticed. The snow was heavier now and there was little light except from the glow of the headlights in front of her.

After about half an hour, she felt the Land Rover slow and turn off the main road. The track was bumpier and she retreated back to her hiding place. After what seemed like an age, she felt the Land Rover slow down and stop. *This must be his home*, she thought.

Very carefully she peeked out from under her cover again. Lights were shining from the front windows of what seemed like a very welcoming bothy. The snow had slowed and although Janey was in the shadows, she had a clear sight of the front door. *I knew it*, she almost shouted out loud but checked herself. There in the doorway was a woman with a small child clinging to her skirt. As Hugh approached, she held out her arms and he reciprocated. The extended hug and affectionate kiss followed by Hugh lifting the child up in his arms told the whole story. He was indeed clearly married. Not just that but he had a child. Janey felt quite sick. Being right didn't make her feel any better. And now she had no clue what to do. The door of the bothy closed behind the happy little family. Gingerly, Janey crawled out from under the smelly tarpaulin and clambered down from the back of the Land Rover. The curtains of the bothy were open. I suppose you can do that with no neighbours to bother with, thought Janey. She crept over to the house, being careful to keep to the shadows. She could just make out the sounds of laughter and a child's voice clamouring for its father's attention she supposed. She carefully peeked into the room. The scene that greeted her made her want to storm in and confront them all. Two children, a girl a good bit older, and the little boy that had greeted Hugh at the door. *How could he?* Janey was livid. A lovely little family and carrying on with Katie. Janey couldn't decide who she felt most sorry for – the pretty wife and children or her best friend. It was too much. No wonder he'd been so furious when Janey had tried to interfere. He clearly had the best of both worlds. A wife and kids tucked away in the middle of nowhere who none of his friends seemed to know about (otherwise surely David or Betty would have said or at least hinted about something) – and a pretty bit on the side who was head over heels about him. Janey sank down out of sight. She had a long walk in front of her with plenty to think about.

She edged to the end of the bothy, again keeping to the shadows. As she started to creep past the Land Rover, she saw Hugh out of the corner of her eye closing the curtains. She froze where she was but he must have caught sight of some movement. Janey looked about her from the Land Rover to the track leading to the main road. He'd easily see her if he was making his way to the front door even if she ran and he'd see the footprints in the light snowfall. Set back from the left hand side of the bothy was a shed and the door was ajar so Janey bolted across to it. It was in the shadow so unless he had a torch, her prints wouldn't be seen and the light snow that had begun to fall would quickly obscure them. She sneaked through the door and tried to look around her. There was hardly any light but she could just make out what looked like large sacks of animal feed. She could fit easily behind them and crouched down trying to calm her thumping heart and gasping breath.

Chapter 52

"Who's there?"

Hugh was standing at the front door. He was sure he'd seen some movement outside. The snow was falling softly and he couldn't make out and shapes. He moved out into the yard in front of the bothy.

"Anyone there?" he called again into the darkness.

The light from the bothy shone out but there was no movement in the yard. He walked round the Land Rover, but there was nothing to be seen.

"Can you see anyone?" a nervous female voice called from the doorway.

"No, could just have been a deer. They'll be coming closer now that the snow's started. Looking for food probably." Hugh turned back towards the door.

"Can you check the shed while you're out there Hugh? I think I might have left the door open after feeding the hens."

"Sure."

Hugh went around the side of the bothy. The shed door was ajar. It was a deer I'll bet, looking for food. At least it's not got into the shed, he thought.

He pulled the door shut and turned the key, and then turned to go back inside to the warmth.

I'll be glad when all this is sorted out; he thought grimly to himself, the duplicity is taking years off my life.

He ached for Katie and knew he would have to face up to things sooner or later. He paused as he got to the door and looked around the yard again. His nerves felt shattered. Keeping up the pretence of normality with his little family indoors was proving a lot tougher then he thought. He knew what he was doing was wrong and he hated himself for being a hypocrite. But he just couldn't help it. He took a deep breath and fixed what he hoped was a relaxed smile on his face and closed the door behind him.

Chapter 53

Well that's done it now, Janey thought. Locked in. *Shit*. She'd heard muffled voices and thought she'd heard someone, probably Hugh's wife, talk about locking the shed. Had Hugh spotted footprints or had the falling snow covered her tracks? Had he gone back in to call for the police about an intruder? Well, she'd soon know.

I suppose then the truth would come out and at least if the police came she'd be safe from Hugh when he found out who the intruder was. He can't suspect it's me, she thought, otherwise he'd have dealt with me right now. I suppose that's something to be grateful for.

It all made sense now – the dodgy Spaniard in Majorca had been right. And not spending a whole night with Katie. And keeping himself detached from his work colleagues. No wonder he never got involved in conversations about family life. And the furious warning he'd given Janey. Well, now everyone would see him for what he was, a cheating bastard. Janey wasn't sure if she was trembling with shock, anger or the cold. At least it was warmish and fairly draught free behind the grain sacks.

She reached for her mobile. No signal, maybe the snow was interfering with the signal. Great. But at least she had a full battery. Just before five in the evening. She crept over to the door and tentatively tried it. Locked fast. Even by the feeble light of her mobile she could see it was the only way out. Janey crept back behind the sacks, pulling one down so that she could sit on it. It was fractionally more comfortable than crouching on the floor. Well, if there was no police this evening and Hugh hadn't deliberately locked her in, she'd have to work out how to get out of here. Even if she had signal, who could she phone? Not John or Lucy at Aigas, they'd think she was mad. She realised then that she'd not be missed because she'd told Lucy she would be in Beauly for the evening. She'd meant to use that excuse to cover her long walk back from Hugh's place. She guessed the drive had been about half an hour give or take, probably six or seven miles away. The twisty roads meant he wouldn't have been driving at any great speed, especially along the track leading to the bothy. *Shit, shit, shit.* What the hell was she going to do? She prayed for him to call the police but as the time crept on, she realised that wasn't going to happen.

Nine o'clock and still no signal. She munched one of the chocolate bars and wondered if it was still snowing. At this rate she'd be stuck here all night. It was very cold in the shed, but there were enough sacks of feed, and what looked like a couple of horse blankets, and she'd wrapped up, so she shouldn't freeze. Janey was thankful the shed appeared weather-proof. She supposed it would have to be with feed being stored. Even still, she could feel the cold. And at least she'd stuck a couple of chocolate bars in her pockets earlier. Janey wasn't sure what she could do except wait it out. Should she call out to Hugh in the morning and risk his reaction? Should she wait for his wife to open the shed door to get the feed out? That could be the best option. Janey could just rush out past her and up the track. Then the police would definitely be called she thought. Then she'd be arrested for trespassing or whatever it was she'd done.

God, it was such a mess. Why couldn't she just have stayed reading in front of the cosy stove in her cabin and stop interfering? It would have worked itself out eventually. She was an idiot. Even the thought that she'd caught Hugh out was of little comfort to her at that moment.

She racked her brains. After what seemed like hours she checked her phone again. It was nearly ten o'clock. Who would help?

David. He'd help her. Of course if he knew about Hugh he might be angry as well but at least he could help get her out of here and away from any angry outburst from Hugh. If only she could get a signal. Janey checked her phone again. One bar, flashed up for the first time since she'd got there. Would that be enough?

She dialled David's number. It seemed to take forever to ring. She heard David answer but the signal was poor and he didn't seem to be able to hear her properly. At least he'd know who called. The phone cut out. *Damn*. She decided to send a text. At least when the signal improved he'd get the text.

help. locked in shed at hughs. found out about his wife. don't call him. help.

Janey wasn't good at texting so capitals were out of the question. She could only sit back and hope David would get the message soon. It was going to be a long night.

Chapter 54

Bloody hell. David woke with a start. Who on Earth was texting him at midnight on a Sunday? He turned over in bed. Well, they could get stuffed till the morning. He dozed off, and then woke again. I suppose it could be urgent, he thought sleepily, otherwise who would bother. Then he remembered the fractured call a couple of hours earlier from Janey. He'd tried to call her back but her phone was either off or out of range. He wondered if the text was to do with her. Only one way to find out. He reached for his mobile and checked the text. It had only just arrived to his phone, but when had Janey sent it?

Now he was wide-awake. He was incredulous. What the hell did she mean? Hugh didn't have a wife. Well, not any more. David knew Hugh had been married once a long time ago. Surely Janey didn't mean she had a problem finding out about Hugh's past. He tried to call her but had no luck. Of course if she really was stuck in a shed at Hugh's, she'd be lucky to get any signal. But stuck in a shed – what the hell was all that about? David had been out to Hugh's bothy when he'd first moved in, but not for a long time and he knew it was far out in the wilds.

Should he really take Janey's message seriously? Maybe it was a wind up. But Janey didn't seem the type. The thought of her freezing in the shed was enough to make him get up.

The cold had got into his bedroom, and he shivered as he pulled on some warm clothes. He knew he should call Hugh, but the tone of the text Janey send was quite odd. What did she mean by not calling Hugh? It was all a bit confusing. David checked the time. Just after midnight.

Maybe he should call John at Aigas. He hated disturbing anyone at this time on a Sunday night, but if Janey was in trouble, John's help would be good. And he had a vehicle that could cope with the track down to Hugh's bothy. David pulled back the curtain and looked out into the night. There was still a fair bit of snow falling and he knew as much as anyone that it could easily be a lot heavier a few miles down the road.

He'd call John.

The 'phone only rang a few times and John answered.

"Hi John, it's David, sorry to call so late."

"No problem David, I was still up. Is there something wrong?"

"I think so. I've had an odd text from Janey."

"Janey, our Janey?"

"Yes, apparently she's locked in a shed at Hugh's place but doesn't want me to contact him. To be honest, I don't really understand what's happened."

"Locked in a shed? Why? How?"

"No idea, but I'm going to go out there. Can I drop my car at your place and borrow a Land Rover?"

"Come straight down. I'll come with you. I think I might know a little about this. But I've no idea why Janey would be there or why she's ended up locked in the shed."

"Thanks, John; I'll see you as soon as I can."

"Drive carefully, David, the snow's getting heavier here."

"Cheers, see you soon, bye."

David got himself into the car after clearing the snow off and set off for Aigas. He felt like he was dreaming. It was spooky driving the road to Aigas with the snow swirling. He only saw one other car on the road all the way down. Only mad fools go driving about in this weather, he thought. He wondered what John had meant when he'd said he might know a bit about what was going on. The night was getting stranger and stranger.

He swung into the drive at Aigas. John was waiting for him in the Land Rover, engine running. David parked and hurried over to the waiting car.

"Hop in, the engine's warm, let's see if we can sort this out." John started down the drive, "I'll explain a bit on the way, but it'll be up to Hugh to fill you in on any details."

David looked confused "What's the big mystery? What the hell is going on John?"

"It's complicated. Hugh has a bit of a situation at home."

"What sort of a situation? Has he got a secret wife stashed away?"

David went on to explain the odd text from Janey in full to John.

"Let's wait till we get there. Hugh can explain."

They drove on through the dark and snow, both with their own thoughts. David was more confused than ever. What were they driving into?

Chapter 55

They arrived at the bothy in darkness, apart from the outside light.

"What now John, should we ring the bell or investigate the shed first?"

As they pulled up to park an upstairs light flicked on.

"There's your answer, David, Hugh must have heard us coming. With any luck he'll recognise the car. I don't fancy being greeted by Hugh wielding one of his shotguns."

They got out of the car and walked through the snow to the front door. It opened as they approached and sure enough there was Hugh complete with gun.

"Thank god it's you two, you had me very worried for a minute." Hugh greeted them with a relieved look. "What's happened to bring you out here at this time of night? Why didn't you call or has the snow brought down the line again?"

"I'm not sure what to say really," John knocked off the snow from his boots as they followed Hugh into the bothy.

"It seems that Janey is locked in your shed."

As Hugh locked up the gun he whirled round to face the two men. "What. Janey in the shed, what…?" Hugh was lost for words.

"I know, I know, but I got a text from her saying she was in your shed and needed help."

"What do you mean; I don't understand any of this. How the hell would she get into the shed?"

"We've really no idea, Hugh, but maybe if we check the shed we'll get to the bottom of this."

"OK, John, let's go."

The three men left the bothy with a torch and went round to the shed. Hugh turned to key, opened the door and John shone the torch into the darkness.

Janey was standing in the corner looking very sheepish.

"I heard the car, thanks for coming."

They all stood for a moment taking in the odd situation.

"I think we should probably go inside and sort this out." John seemed to take command as the others seemed to have lost the power of speech.

They trudged back to the bothy. The snow had stopped and sparkled crisply under the light of the torch.

They trooped into the front room where Hugh's wife was tending to a pot of tea. She looked startled to see Janey with them.

"I heard your voice John, and thought you might need a cuppa."

Janey was startled by her Glaswegian accent, but said nothing. She was feeling very uneasy. Hugh's wife clearly knew John.

"I'll get another cup." Hugh's wife shot a furtive look at Janey and retreated to the kitchen. The atmosphere was tense.

"So Janey, what's this all about? How did you manage to get locked in Hugh's shed? I think you owe us all an explanation." John sat in one of the armchairs and the rest followed suit. Hugh's wife came in with a cup and quietly poured them all some tea. John's tone wasn't accusing or judging, just concerned.

Hugh looked fit to explode, he could hardly contain himself. "You couldn't help yourself, Janey, could you? Interfering with things you know nothing about." He glared at Janey..

Janey took a deep breath. "I'm so sorry for all the fuss. I didn't mean for all this to happen."

"For all what to happen?" David had found his voice and Hugh's expression looked thunderous. He started to speak but John chipped in.

"Let Janey explain it all and maybe we'll get to the bottom of this."

Janey was aware of Hugh's wife sitting in a chair at the table at the back of the room. "I was going to follow Hugh to his house," she started, stopped, then continued "I thought he might see me following him in one of the estate cars so I thought I'd hide in the back of the Land Rover, check the situation out and walk back to Aigas."

"Check the bloody situation?" Hugh spluttered but again John cut in.

"Let her finish Hugh, let her finish." John leaned towards Janey, "What exactly were you checking and why?"

Janey was so glad of his calm and encouraging smile. But she was also conscious that what she was about to say could cause world war three between Hugh and his wife. "Hugh's been seeing my friend Katie. I went to Majorca and saw a picture of him on a scuba-diving advertising board, and the man there told me he'd gone back to Scotland to be with his wife." She didn't dare look at Hugh's wife so addressed John alone. "I suspected he had some secret, because some of his behaviour seemed odd so I thought I'd follow him home to see if he was married."

The words all came tumbling out and Janey knew they sounded really feeble.

"Married, you thought I was bloody married." Hugh exploded. "You stupid interfering little bitch, you've ruined everything."

Janey saw red at his outburst. "If you hadn't been cheating on your wife with my best friend none of this would have happened. You've only got yourself to blame. Don't yell at me just because I've found out your little secret." She glanced at Hugh's wife who'd gone so pale Janey thought she was going to faint.

"Calm down you two." John stood up and tried to soothe the situation. He turned to Hugh. "I think you're going to have to explain to David and Janey, Hugh. Tell them everything and maybe they'll understand. I'm sure once they know all the facts they'll keep your confidence."

It was Janey and David's turn to look confused.

"I don't know, John. It could ruin everything." Hugh put his head in his hands.

His wife came over and squeezed his shoulder. "I think we're going to have to share this, Hugh, I'm OK with it. These people are you friends. It'll all be over soon anyway and the truth will come out."

Hugh looked up at her and covered her hand with his. "Are you sure you're OK with this, Isabel?"

Isabel, so that's what his wife's name is, thought Janey, how can she be so clam about all of this. She's behaving like she knew all about it in some strange way. If it were me, I'd want to bloody kill him.

Hugh started to speak. "I need to know that I can swear you all to secrecy. Obviously I'll have to tell Katie too." Hugh looked around to see that they were all listening.

Now Janey was really confused. She was beginning to have the growing feeling that her suspicions were way out of line.

"Isabel is not my wife, Janey…"

"But I saw you kissing her." Janey blurted out.

Hugh cut back in. "She's my sister. She's been here for eighteen months. She's in hiding from her ex-husband. He tried to kill her and abduct the children. He's been a complete bastard to her over the years…"

"No need to go into details, Hugh," Isabel cut in, "I'm sure they get the picture."

"Sorry Issy, yes, he's on remand awaiting trial at the moment. A bit of a Glasgow gangster I'm afraid. Quite turned my wee sister's head." Hugh shot a look up at Isobel and she raised her eyebrows wistfully.

"Yes, I was quite taken in, I'm afraid, but at least I have two lovely kids. I have to look on the bright side."

"He found Isabel in the first two refuges she was in, so because his dodgy contacts wouldn't be able to track me down because they didn't know we were still in contact, I was able to appear distanced from my sister as I'd been working abroad and we had little contact, the police thought she'd be safe here. John's known all about it and so does Betty, so that if anyone did enquire about me we could act straight away.

Isabel's ex is in prison on remand, awaiting trial for violent domestic abuse."

"God, Hugh I'm so sorry." Janey found herself close to tears at her stupidity. "I'm sorry I jumped to the wrong conclusion." She looked to Isabel, "I know it's no comfort to you, and I've behaved insensitively, but I've been through a relationship with an abusive husband. So I can try to understand what you're going through. I am so sorry." Janey couldn't help the tears rolling down her cheeks. Janey was truly shocked. She hardly dare look at them all. The turmoil of emotion chasing around in her head was almost too much to take. If anyone should know how scared Isabel felt, it was her. Janey too had experience of a violent husband. Thankfully her ex didn't give her any trouble anymore. He'd tried, but Janey knew that all she had to do was complain about it in the right ear and he'd be out of a job. She knew Nick wouldn't ever have coped with that. He'd tried very hard to discredit Janey when she started telling folk about the real reason she'd kicked him out, but it hadn't worked. His poor reputation amongst his fellow officers meant that they probably saw through him. A quiet chat with one of his superiors had taught Janey that. No, she'd taken the easy option and kept quiet, deciding not to press charges. Mainly for the sake of the children and at least it had guaranteed that the kids got maintenance payments. Janey really felt for Isabel. It must be terrifying to have to go into hiding from your ex-husband. What a fool she'd been. Janey just wanted the ground to open and swallow her up. How would she ever get over this? And all the trouble she'd caused; they'd want her on the next train south; that was for sure. Her hands were shaking, and she felt heartsick. Isabel came over and sat on the arm of Janey's chair. She put her hand on Janey's shoulder and spoke.

"No we don't hate you." Isabel was smiling at her. "Katie is lucky to have such a good friend to look after her interests. Just like I'm lucky to have such a good big brother to look out for me. I think Hugh was protecting me by not telling me about Katie. He knew I would worry that our hiding place would be found if anyone else knew."

"I even had my suspicions about you, you know, Janey." Hugh was looking directly at her now. "When you started talking about Oban and how your ex was in the police, I thought maybe Isabel's ex-husband had tracked me down and sent you to dig for more information. Lucky for you, John was sure it was a coincidence, otherwise I'd have moved on with Issy and the kids. I lived in Oban with my ex-wife. All her family came from there." Hugh looked tired and ashen faced. He looked at Issy. "You're right; I knew you'd worry if you knew I'd met someone I cared about. So I decided not to tell Katie about you. It's been killing me keeping things from you both. I just thought it was safer that way."

Issy went over to Hugh and hugged him. "You spend too much time worrying. Maybe Katie is just what you need to get on with your life. I'm pleased for you." She sat down on the arm of his chair with her hand on his shoulder.

"I saw your picture in Majorca when I went on a holiday there. The diver guy said you'd gone back to Scotland to be with your wife." Janey thought she might as well get the whole story off her chest. "And then when you wouldn't spend the whole night with Katie…" Janie tailed off, it sounded so absurd now that she knew the truth.

"I expect they came to their own conclusions in Majorca, but I left to come back here to help Isabel and the kids. They were only six and four at the rime. And when I met Katie, I couldn't leave Isabel and her children all night. She was nervous enough, but I had to put her needs first." Hugh paused and looked at Janey. "Do you think Katie will understand? And will you keep quiet?" Hugh sent a stern look to Janey. "I'm so mad at you for interfering, but we're going to have to work together for the next while."

"I'm sure she will understand, and she'll keep quiet." John interrupted the conversation.

Janey had another confession to make. "I told Katie about my suspicions. That's why we had such a row. I'm sorry."

"She did say something. But I'm sure she'll come around. I'll call her in the morning." Hugh eventually smiled weakly at Janey.

"Well, speaking of morning, it's here already and as it's a working day, I think we all need some rest. Let's get together tomorrow." John stood as he spoke.

"I'm rarely stuck for words but I don't know what to say." David rose from the armchair. "This has been some night. Full of revelations." He turned to Hugh, "You could have trusted me you know. I wouldn't have said anything."

Hugh stood and touched David's arm. "I know, you're a good friend. We just felt the fewer folk that knew the better. I didn't mean to leave you out."

"I understand and I promise I won't say a thing to anyone. Maybe Janey and I can come over for supper with the two of you sometime, just for the company, I mean." David glanced at Janey as he spoke but she was clearly thinking far away thoughts and missed the invitation.

"Come on you two, let these folk get to bed. David has a few miles to drive after we get back to Aigas. Unless you want to walk Janey?" John's remark made them all smile and broke the tension.

"It's fine, John," Even Janey was able to smile. "a lift sounds just grand."

They said their goodbyes with Janey still trying to offer her apologies and climbed into John's Land Rover.

There was mostly silence on the journey back to Aigas. The world looked lovely. The snow sparkled in the headlights and the snow-covered trees and bushes gave their own display of twinkling in the darkness.

Once back at Aigas, Janey mumbled her apologies once again to David and John and hurried towards her cabin. She just wanted to crawl under the nearest stone. She'd been so stupid and caused so much grief. Would any of them forgive her? She'd probably have to leave Aigas now. The thought appalled her. Although she appreciated that her intentions were sound, she knew she'd caused a lot of trouble. And for her to have upset Isabel when Janey knew some of the heartache Isabel was going through. How she wished she could turn the clock back. But what was done was done and she'd have to face the consequences. She would have loved to go and see Isabel and offer her all the support she could. But that was hardly likely now.

She really hoped Hugh, John and David would forgive her stupid interference. The thought of David brought a slow smile to her lips. She'd been very glad to see him tonight.

David had been a good friend to her. Maybe she'd been too hard on him. But she was in a quandary after meeting Iain. She knew who'd had the most dramatic effect on her. With Iain there was none of the slight unease she felt with David. Still, she hoped he'd still want to see her next week to sort out her money situation. He might change his mind after the problems she'd caused Hugh. Janey hoped not. And what Katie would say, god only knew. She'd think about it all tomorrow.

Despite the hour, she intended to soak in a bath before sleep claimed her, and despite the problems she'd caused, she felt as though a huge weight had been lifted and she felt exhausted.

John and David watched her go.

"An eventful night all round. Don't be too hard on her for causing all the fuss." John shook David's hand as he spoke.

"Give her a chance to get over this. Then ask her out for god's sake. You look like a lovesick puppy every time you look at her."

David laughed, "That obvious eh? Trouble is, I don't even think she's even noticed me."

"Give her time. She called you for help remember, no one else. Take it slowly. She's here for a couple of weeks yet, although I think she'll need some persuading to stay. She probably thinks we'll ask her to leave in the morning, but that's not going to happen. You see, David, I know quite a lot about Janey, things she'll tell you in her own good time. I have a feeling she'll take this too hard. She'll need her own kind of support and we'll be there for her. She'll need the next wee while to recover and get back on track, but I've no doubt she will. Aigas is a wonderful place, healing is good here. She'll be fine. Come round for dinner and join in with the guests tomorrow night. Janey's working. She makes a mean sticky toffee pudding. And we're to have a few clear crisp nights this week. Let the romance of Aigas guide you."

"You're a good man, John. And I have a good feeling about Janey. I don't blame her for doing what she did. She was looking out for a friend. That sort of loyalty is rare. Although it's caused a bit of a problem for Hugh and Isabel, I admire that quality in Janey. Thanks. See you tomorrow... well that's today now. See you later." David headed for his car, his mind full of thoughts about the evening past. But more so he was thinking about Janey. She was a hell of a woman and he wanted to know a lot more about her.

David drove carefully back through the snow to Beauly. The night was crisp and clear now. He contemplated the crazy evening. He also thought about how the mad lowland lass had got under his skin. The thought of Janey made him smile. For the first time in a long time, he knew he really needed to get her to like him. But John was right; he'd have to give her time. But she had called him, David, for help. That appealed to his protective nature. How lovely it would be to have someone to care for and to care for him back. He hardly dared hope. Maybe seeing her next week would help. He hoped she'd stay on at Aigas for the rest of her time and not feel she had to run away home to Edinburgh because of the night's events. Janey seemed vulnerable and that was just the kind of woman David liked. He'd be able to be in control, give her all the things she'd love, romantic and generous gestures that would win her over. And she had money she was going to trust him with. David was looking forward to seeing Janey again.

He thought about what John had said. The Aigas Magic. He'd work his charm on Janey and maybe the Magic would work for him.

Chapter 56

Janey felt like such a fool. She was all snuggled up in her cosy bed after a long soak in the bath, reliving the evening. The snow was heavy now and she watched it fall through the window of her bedroom. In the silence of the countryside, she thought she could hear the show falling softly on the ground. Big, white flakes that sparkled in the light of the lamp beside her snug cabin. Lindsay was away for the night and Janey was glad. She just wanted to be alone with all her jumbled thoughts. She'd got it all wrong with Hugh, suspecting him when he was only helping his family. She only hoped Katie would forgive her for all the trouble she'd caused. John had been so understanding and reassured her that her job was still there. Things would be awkward between her and Hugh for a while she supposed, but she'd sworn to keep his secret and even offered to speak to his sister Issy, if she needed support. Hugh was going to call Katie to explain everything and ask for her to keep his confidence. There was no question of that. Katie was loyal and Janey hoped they could repair their friendship.

After all, Janey had been through it all with a violent and controlling husband. She just hoped that when and if she embarked on another relationship, she'd recognise the potential 'controller' before she fell in too deep. Janey thought about David. He'd been a real help this evening. Janey quite liked him, but felt there was something about him that wasn't quite right. His cheeky, cheerful manner that everyone seemed to admire, was disarming. What if he wanted more than to be her financial advisor? She'd just have to be careful. There was no way Janey wanted to be involved with another controlling man. She was her own woman now and she had proved it. On the other hand, Iain the GP had definite potential. And he came from Edinburgh and would be there by the time she went home. Janey was quite certain that if he called her while she was here, she'd definitely take him up on his dinner invitation. Life was looking up. Whatever her next move would be or whatever her next job would be, she'd face it with all the strength she'd found from this magical place.

The Aigas magic was well known for changing lives.

⚥ EDINBURGH WOMEN'S AID

"Having the courage to contact Women's Aid changed my life. There is amazing support for women in abusive relationships, no judging and just complete understanding. They provide the space to re-build. I am donating a pound from every book sale to support their fantastic work." – LJB Fraser

About Women's Aid Edinburgh

What we do:

Edinburgh Women's Aid is an all women, confidential organisation which provides information, support and, where appropriate, refuge accommodation, for women and any accompanying children affected by domestic abuse. No woman or child should be subjected to domestic abuse. If it is happening to you, please remember, it's not your fault and we can help. If you can contact us safely, please get in touch with Edinburgh Women's Aid on 0131 315 8110. Women and children accessing our services have a range of choices in how to interact with our service. The support provided includes emotional support as well as information and choices concerning domestic abuse, such as housing options, benefits, welfare rights and legal issues.

Drop-in service and Phone Support: 0131 315 8110 - 4 Cheyne Street, Edinburgh EH4 1JB
Mon: 1pm – 3pm (phone support from 10am)
Tue: 10am – 3pm
Wed: 10am – 3pm
Thu: 2pm – 7pm (phone support from 10am)
Fri: 10am – 3pm
Sat: 10am – 1pm